Sarah was looking at the Big Island. Right beyond the rocky shoreline, the thick trees began. It was dark and shadowy and somehow intriguing.

"We've never been there," she said, pointing to the island. "I wonder what it's like. We've seen everything else on the lake, but never the Big Island. You've never been there, have you?"

He shook his head.

"Wouldn't you like to? I mean just a quick look? I hear there's a house there somewhere."

"Not a house, a hotel, but it's been shut up for years."

"A hotel? That's even better," Sarah was starting to get excited about this idea. "That's got to be our challenge this year."

Every year since they were little kids they had given themselves a challenge, something they had never done before. Last year it had been swimming the point, a right of passage to swim across the lake. Other years it had been riding the falls on White River or hiking into Milford or jumping into the sand quarry.

"Challenge?" he looked at the island and then back at Sarah. "Come on Ramsey, aren't we a little old for that?"

"So call it something else." She was suddenly embarrassed. "I want to know what's on the island. I'd like to see the hotel."

The Secrets
of Loon Lake

The Secrets
of Loon Lake

a mystery by
J. D. Shaw

Tiny Satchel Press
Philadelphia

Tiny Satchel Press
    311 West Seymour Street
    Philadelphia, PA 19144
    tinysatchelpress@gmail.com
    www.tinysatchelpress.com

Distributed by
    Bella Distribution Services
    P.O. Box 10543
    Tallahassee, FL 32302
    1-800-729-4992

Tiny Satchel Press Publisher: Victoria A. Brownworth
Production coordination: Chris Angelucci
Book design: Judith Redding
Cover production: Jennifer Mercer
Tiny Satchel Press logo: Chris Angelucci

Printed in the United States of America.

First edition.

ISBN 978-0-9845318-0-6

To Victoria Brownworth,
without whom this book would not exist.
Her friendship, encouragement, and truly marvelous insight
into writing have been a blessing.

1

According to Sarah Ramsey, summer officially began when the car made the turn in the dirt path that wound through the woods. That was her first glimpse of Loon Lake.

Three minutes later, when they arrived at the cottage, her sister, Jennifer, bounded out of the car before it came to a complete stop. She had to check up on her friends. Like Sarah didn't have friends? But then, she didn't seem to count in this family and drama-queen Jennifer had become such an expert at causing a scene that they all bowed to her wishes.

Which left Sarah to help her mother unpack the car and get the cottage set up for the summer. It took awhile, but she couldn't just leave her mother to do it by herself. Even if her sister was too self-centered to notice that Mom wasn't Mom these days, Sarah was well aware of what was going on. Her mother could manage moments of pasted-on enthusiasm, but when she thought nobody was looking, she was visibly sad.

The cottage was small and at least there weren't any mice in the mattresses this year, so finally Sarah could put on her swimsuit, slip a sweatshirt over her head, and make her way down to the dock.

The motor-boat had been put in the water, the motor already attached as promised. Her dad had called John at the marina. Dad hadn't driven up with them this year. First time ever. Things were not going well with Sarah's parents. Dad had kissed his daughters goodbye; he hadn't kissed their mother. The big "D" word had not been mentioned, but it hovered.

Sarah's dog, Conrad, jumped into the boat and perched himself on the small front seat like some kind of doggie-figurehead. He was fairly large, part Husky and part Lab, and he looked like he'd topple over into the water at any minute, but he never did. Every other year, it had been Sarah and her dad and Conrad who had gone to look for the raft, which always got washed away in the winter. It was their way of saying hello to the lake. Sarah felt compelled to keep that tradition, with or without her dad. Tradition was important; everyone on the lake appreciated what a special place it was. They knew there weren't many unspoiled lakes left anymore. They were determined that Loon would stay just the way it had always been. Sarah's dad was chairman of the board of that no-change philosophy. He had ingrained it in them. He had grown up on the lake and loved it as much as she did. But the very fact that he wasn't here was a rather big break in tradition, wasn't it? She didn't want to be mad at her father. He was a great guy. She had always been a daddy's girl. And although she knew parents didn't pick favorites, she felt like her dad's favorite. Maybe her sister did too, but Sarah and her dad liked the same kinds of things, and he used to be fun and funny and sometimes downright silly. Lately, that part of him seemed to be missing. Their house was now capital "S" serious.

She thought it was ironic, her dad probably needed the lake this summer more than he ever had before, with what was going on in his life, and he wasn't here. Her mother loved the lake too, but she had married into it and that wasn't quite the same. Sarah had thought that once they all got up here everything would settle down and get back to the way it was. She had never imagined her dad would stay away. Not that he ever spent the whole summer, he had to work, but every weekend he was here and he always managed several weeks, and he definitely always came up and got everything turned on and ready-to-go.

The motor didn't start at the first pull. Sarah practically wrenched off her arm before it caught. That made her mad too. Her dad was supposed to be doing this. Their boat wasn't any kind of fancy speed boat, it was just a rowboat with a motor on the back. There was nothing fancy about Loon Lake, no white-carpeted McMansions like those popping up on the other lakes in the area. Here, people liked their little cottages with the linoleum floors where kids could stand and drip in their swim suits.

She pulled the boat into the middle of the lake, getting used to steering again. It felt good, letting the wind blow her hair, hearing the bow slap the water, feeling the power and speed under her hand. She kept her eyes out for the raft, but she was reveling in the ride. She spotted her sister, hanging out with all her friends on Tommy Emmerson's dock. Actually she heard the music first, booming across the water. There must have been some sort of strange star alignment going on when her sister was born. There were so many kids her age around the lake. At one time it was something like twelve; now a couple of them were already in college and not coming up for the whole summer anymore. But there they were, all crowded on the dock, gyrating to the beat of music so loud Sarah couldn't tell if it was rap or rock, the boys and the girls all over each other. From this distance, it looked like some kind of weird ritual. At least her sister hadn't had time to put on her bikini yet. She saw Rachel Young there, dancing with more grace than the others. Rachel was nice, she actually acknowledged Sarah's existence.

There was an almost even split between the sexes with the group. Occasionally two would pair up, but usually they went around in one big gang. There were only two kids Sarah's age on the lake, Robbie Rearden and Jake Hawkins; no other girls. They were all fourteen, Robbie almost fifteen, Sarah in the middle, and Jake would have just had his birthday. The older kids never wanted them hanging around, so Sarah had become one of the boys a long time ago.

She got beyond the booming music and started to feel the peaceful feeling she always had out on the water. This was the place where she really felt like she belonged. She noticed things here that she didn't pay attention to anywhere else. She watched some fish jump out of the water and heard a flock of birds shrieking in some trees. There was so much wildlife, just about everything, except the loons that gave the lake its name. They were here once, but Sarah had never seen any. She had read about them, though. They weighed about nine pounds and had a wing span of five feet and red eyes. She always wished she could see one. But they were gone now. Things did change at the lake, and sometimes there was nothing anyone could do to stop it.

Loon was big for a mud-bottom lake, about seventy-five cottages scattered around it, separated from each other by woods. There were some islands here and there, most of them small, like Sunken Island, in front of Sarah's cottage, that some years was there and some years not. The one impressive island was in the middle of the lake. There were only two rules to be obeyed during the summer. Never swim alone and never go to the Big Island. It was private property and it was posted, and it had a rocky shore line that made pulling a boat up there dangerous. It also had an abundance of what the lake people called "bloodsuckers" and other people called leeches. There was nothing worse than getting ready for bed at night and pulling off your sneakers only to find a bloodsucker that had been feasting between your toes since early morning. Kids learned to swim early at Loon Lake. They really didn't want to touch the bottom.

So Sarah hoped she wouldn't find the raft washed up on the Big Island. She wanted something simple, not wedged between rocks, not caught in weeds, not anywhere that she had to stand in the water and deal with muck and bloodsuckers.

Of course, no such luck. The storms had been fierce this last winter and the raft was on the north side of the Big Island, caught between rocks about two feet from shore, farther away than it had ever drifted before.

Everyone put markers on their rafts. Sarah's had a big-faded-red R for Ramsey painted across the top. And Conrad, the world's smartest dog, was already barking at it.

She did a pretty good job of killing the motor at just the right second and letting the boat glide up to the raft. Then she pulled off her sweatshirt, took off her sneakers, and hopped over the side of the boat, rope in hand. It was like stepping into ice cubes; this was only June, after all. The mud oozed between her toes and pictures of leeches danced in her head. Conrad was directing her with barks.

She got the rope tied on just fine and got back into the boat and into her sweatshirt, did a quick check of her toes for bloodsuckers, and even managed to get the motor started. But the raft wouldn't budge. It was big, meant for four or five people to lie down on it at the same time, and it was heavy and unwieldy. Okay. Now she really needed her dad. There was a bunch of anger riding around in her stomach. For the first time she wished she had one of those new inflatable trampoline rafts that were showing up in front of cottages these days. But, oh no, not with her traditionalist dad. Up until right now she would have described herself as a traditionalist too. Maybe she needed to do some rethinking.

"Ramsey, about time you got up here." The voice startled her. She had been so caught up in her frustration she hadn't even noticed the canoe that was heading toward her.

"Hi Robbie," she called. "Just the guy I wanted to see."

"Got a problem?" he asked.

"You think?" she answered sarcastically.

He swung his canoe alongside her boat and threw her a rope. Then he stood up and took off his sweatshirt, ready to help.

Wow. What had happened to him? He had been her height last summer. Can a person grow more than a foot over the winter? And those shoulders. Where had they come from? Robbie Rearden had suddenly turned into big-time hot. His hair was light brown but it would turn blond as the summer went on. He had really blue eyes, cobalt blue. They'd look even more blue when he got his normal tan. Even his face, the same but not the same, stronger somehow. She knew she was staring at him. Robbie and Jake had been her summer friends since before she could remember, probably since they were in diapers. But this guy—who was he? It gave her a funny feeling, thinking of him the way she was thinking of him. She had always had a comfort zone with Robbie. She didn't feel that comfort right now. It made for an awkward moment.

"Good God, Robbie, have you been lifting weights or something?" she asked.

He was about to step out of his boat. He paused and looked down at her. "Um, people don't actually call me Robbie anymore," he said, looking a bit sheepish.

"Except that it's your name."

"Yeah, but my friends call me Robert now, or Rob's okay."

She tried it out on her tongue. It didn't fit.

"How come?" she asked. Her question sounded dumb to her own ears. She wasn't used to thinking before she talked, not with Robbie.

"Come on, Ramsey. Robbie? I'm not three years old anymore."

She couldn't argue with that, not with those shoulders.

He stepped into the water. The cold didn't seem to bother him at all. Working his way around the sides of the raft, he reached down and pulled up hunks of weeds. Then he started rocking the raft back and forth. It was a flat wooden platform raised up on pontoons, and even though it tipped, it was still heavy. But maybe that weight lifting, or whatever, was working. With one fierce push the raft came free.

"Great," she shouted. "Robbie–excuse me–Rob, that's great."

His grin hadn't changed.

He climbed into her boat and was looking at his feet. Sure enough, there was a bloodsucker on the bottom of his big toe. She handed him the salt shaker they always kept in the boat. Luckily it was still there from last summer. Nothing was pouring out of the little holes anymore. Rob took off the rusty top and spread some salt on the leech and it instantly curled up and died. Sarah liked most things in nature, but she couldn't get up any empathy for anything as gross as a bloodsucker.

However, she wasn't watching him pick up the creature and throw it into the water, she was looking at the Big Island. Right beyond the rocky shoreline, the thick trees began. It was dark and shadowy and somehow intriguing.

"We've never been there," she said, pointing to the island. "I wonder what it's like. We've seen everything else on the lake, but never the Big Island. You've never been there, have you?"

He shook his head.

"Wouldn't you like to? I mean just a quick look? I hear there's a house there somewhere."

"Not a house, a hotel, but it's been shut up for years."

"A hotel? That's even better," Sarah was starting to get excited about this idea. "That's got to be our challenge this year."

Every year since they were little kids they had given themselves a challenge, something they had never done before. Last year it had been swimming the point, a right of passage to swim across the lake. Other years it had been riding the falls on White River or hiking into Milford or jumping into the sand quarry.

"Challenge?" he looked at the island and then back at Sarah. "Come on Ramsey, aren't we a little old for that?"

"So call it something else." She was suddenly embarrassed. "I want to know what's on the island. I'd like to see the hotel."

He shrugged, he obviously wasn't interested. He stood up and grabbed his sweatshirt again. He was a fabulous swimmer and he had a swimmer's body. His stomach muscles rippled as he stretched his arms to pull the sweatshirt over his head. Sarah looked away. This was her friend, Robbie. She wanted to keep thinking of him like that. And at the same time she didn't want to. And she was more than embarrassed by his lack of interest in her island idea, she felt hurt by it.

"I bet Jake will want to go. Is he here yet?"

"Yeah, Hawkins is here." He sat down on the middle seat again and reached forward, rubbing Conrad's ears. If a dog could purr, that particular gesture would be Conrad's turn-on point.

"So, Sarah, how was your winter?" he asked.

That stopped her. He usually didn't call her Sarah. Years ago the boys had started using each other's last names and then they started doing it to her. She liked it, membership in the club or something. For herself, she pretty much stuck to their first names, she didn't know why. But there was something nice about the way he said Sarah. She actually wanted him to say it again.

"Pretty good winter," she answered his question. But she wondered what he'd think of her if he knew her in the winter. It was such a different world. Would he look at her friends and know her for the nerd she really was? She was a member of the science club, for God's sake. Not that she would apologize for that. She liked it. They had been studying forensics this last year and it was really interesting. But she looked at Rob and knew he'd definitely be one of the cool kids at his school. That was something else she had never thought about before. Sarah was not particularly impressed by coolness. She had observed her sister, whose lifetime ambition was to be cool and popular. It seemed, to Sarah, to be a very restrictive life style. Jennifer's winter friends had a vocabulary consisting of about six phrases, mostly concerning the weirdness of anyone who wasn't them. And if any one of them, by some freak of nature, should ever come up with an original thought, Sarah was sure it would result in instant ejection from the group.

But Rob and Jake and Sarah were summer friends, they didn't even e-mail in the winter. It was like their friendship was attached to the lake. Rob lived on the other side of the city from Sarah and Jake lived in a different town altogether. Each year their friendship waited for summer and took off just where they had left it.

"So how come you're getting the raft by yourself? It's a pretty big job. How come your dad's not doing it?" Rob asked her.

"He didn't come up with us." Sarah didn't want to talk about that.

"When's he coming?" Rob asked, pulling on the rope that held his canoe.

"I don't know. Who cares?"

"I care," he said as he was climbing into his boat. "I like your dad."

"You never even talk to my dad."

"Actually, I do. I've talked to him a lot. I've always been kind of fascinated with him being a criminal attorney, that sounds so cool. I told him I might like to do that, like go to law school. And ever since, he's been telling me some really great stuff about his cases."

"You are such a liar. My dad never discusses his cases. He's not even supposed to. There's that confidentiality thing."

"Maybe he doesn't discuss them with you, but he's told me about some neat trials and weird stuff that's happened."

A shot of anger, complete with pain, twisted up Sarah's stomach. This was the last straw. She was already mad at her dad. Her resentment had been building all day and her dad wasn't here and there was nowhere to direct that anger except at Rob.

"You think you're such a big deal, Robert Rearden, too old for challenges, too old for any fun. Well, excuse me, I'm sorry my father isn't here to have more mature conversations with you than I'm capable of. Maybe you should go join your brother and my sister and their friends. You even sound like my sister with her stuck-up voice."

"Where's all this coming from?" Rob asked, sitting himself back in his canoe and looking at Sarah as if she had gone insane.

She didn't know where it was coming from. This was the day she looked forward to all year, and so far it was a total disaster. Why couldn't Rob just be Robbie? Nothing was turning out like she had expected.

She was furious. There were tears pricking the back of her eyes. She could hear herself sounding infantile, but her anger was driving her mouth. She needed to get away before she said anything else stupid.

"Don't even talk to me, I'm going to find Jake." She threw him his rope, pulled the motor cord, and roared off, almost capsizing his canoe with her wake and the swinging, unstable raft she was pulling. It wasn't totally on purpose; at least, she didn't think it was.

2

Sarah found that it wasn't easy steering the boat with the weight of the raft jerking it from side to side. She had never done this part before, her dad had always driven home. It wasn't helping that her stomach was still tied up in knots. Who did Robbie Rearden think he was? She couldn't accept the idea that her father had talked about something with Robbie that he always refused to talk about with her. And she was also beginning to worry about how she was going to get the raft attached to the anchor — that was definitely a two-person job.

It did occur to her that if she hadn't yelled at Robbie, he would be here, but, at the moment, she needed her anger more than his help.

If, on her way across the lake, she had looked toward Jake Hawkins's cottage, she would have seen him getting into his kayak. He saw her, but she was too far away to hear his call. He finished putting on his life jacket and getting himself settled. It looked like she was heading home and she was struggling. He watched, as the unwieldy raft swayed from one side to the other, taking Sarah's boat with it, like a tail wagging a dog.

It gave him some satisfaction to see her struggle. The thing about old Ramsey was that she always did everything a little too well, a little better than he could do himself. Not that he didn't like her, she wasn't all silly and giggly like the girls at school. She was actually interesting. He had been looking forward to her getting up here, especially since Rob had changed so much over the winter. All of a sudden he felt like a jerk next to Rob, like a short, skinny, stupid kid or something. It wasn't fair when some kids shot up like that. Not that Rob had seemed to notice. But Jake didn't like standing next to him anymore. They used to fool around with each other, give each other a shove or a punch in the ribs, especially if they happened to be on the edge of a dock or something. Jake didn't think there'd be any more of that kind of fooling around. It would be way too one-sided. And there was something about Rob's attitude that wouldn't have included pushing, anyway.

He aimed his boat toward Sarah's, but she had already reached her cottage. He saw her turn off the motor and throw the anchor out about forty feet from shore, just about perfect for where the raft usually was. She dove into the water and was down there for a long time. She had always been able to hold her breath forever, something else she did better than Jake.

She came up a couple of times for air. He called out once, but she didn't hear him. And she dove quickly back down again. He stopped paddling when his boat was next to hers and watched her down there. She had found the raft anchor and chain and was trying to tie the raft rope to it. That couldn't be easy while treading underwater.

Finally she started for the surface, checking to see where her boat was, so she wouldn't hit her head. There were two shadows. She swam around the two boats and when her head came up out of the water she was gasping for breath. It took her a minute before she climbed up on the raft and could speak.

"How long have you been here?" she asked Jake, still breathing heavily.

"Look enough to see you floundering around down there," he said.

"So why didn't you help me?"

"I've got my own work to do, why should I do yours too?"

Sarah actually smiled. "At least *you* haven't changed," she said.

"So, you've seen *Sir Robert*." Jake drew out the name. He had a bit of a donkey bray when he laughed. And even this small chuckle had the donkey element. It always made Sarah crack up.

"Yes, I've seen Mr. Rearden. He acts like a middle-aged man or something."

"He won a state swim championship this year. Give him time, he'll get over himself, especially up here."

"That's a beautiful boat, when did you get that?" Sarah was looking at the shiny red kayak.

"I got it for my birthday. Neat, huh?"

"Your parents sure give better birthday presents than mine do," she said with a degree of jealousy.

"It comes with a lot of conditions," Jake said. "So how come Rob didn't help you with the raft?"

"I got mad at him. I thought I had our challenge for this year, exploring the Big Island, but he wanted no part of it."

"Cool," said Jake. "That would be fun. And don't worry about Rearden, he'll come around. When? Let's do it tonight."

"Not at night, we couldn't see anything, and besides it would be creepy at night," Sarah said.

"We can't go in the daytime. Too many boats on the water. Somebody would see us and stop us. There's all those no trespassing signs."

"True. We'll go early in the morning," said Sarah, stretching out on the raft.

"Yeah, sunrise. Whenever time that is. Before the first fishing boats are out."

"I think the sunrise is about five o'clock right now." Sarah closed her eyes, looking perfectly relaxed.

"Whoa, that's early. And it's just like you to know that stuff." Jake frowned, a bit disgruntled. "So, Ramsey, did you get all 'A's again this year?"

"Am I expected to apologize for the fact that I have some working brain cells?"

"Yeah, you are. Not cool. Anyway, let's go tomorrow morning. I'll get Rearden to go. We'll use his canoe. It's big and quiet."

"It's funny, isn't it," Sarah said, opening her eyes and turning her head to look across the water. "That island's been in front of us all our lives, and we've never been there. How come nobody goes there?"

"The older kids go there sometimes, to drink beer and stuff." He raised his eyebrows suggestively, but Sarah wasn't even looking at him, so he climbed on the raft, holding onto his boat with his feet.

"How do you know the older kids go there?" Sarah closed her eyes again.

"I've seen lights, like flashlights. You can see a different side from my cottage. And I've seen a fire, like a bonfire, way off in the woods there."

"You've never mentioned that before." Sarah raised her head enough to look at him.

"I'm not a snitch. You're not supposed to be there." Jake lay down, full out, on the raft beside Sarah.

"Feels good, doesn't it?" Sarah said. "After a winter, I love feeling the first rays. It's like your bones need it or something."

"Yeah, it feels good," agreed Jake. He relaxed, and that was when he lost his foot grip on his boat.

"Grab it, Ramsey," he shouted.

"You grab it," said Sarah. "I've got my own work to do, why should I do yours?"

Jake aimed a dirty look in her direction, but she had her eyes closed again. Then he dove into the water, life jacket still on, which made him bounce right back up like some kind of bobblehead. Of course, Sarah had opened her eyes for that.

"Good God," he shouted. "This water is freezing."

Sarah laughed and watched him grab his boat and get back in with an ungraceful thump. He paddled back to the raft.

"Okay. Tomorrow morning, we conquer the Big Island. Be at my dock at five. This is going to be cool," said Jake.

3

The worst thing about summer was the fact that Sarah and her sister shared a bedroom. The only thing that saved them from outright murder was that they didn't spend any time there except to sleep. But therein lay the problem. Sarah had lost the coin toss this year, she had the top bunk.

And now she had to get up at the crack of dawn and not wake Jennifer when she climbed down.

She had a digital watch with an alarm, but even that might wake Jennifer. Not that she would care where Sarah was going, she didn't even notice she was alive. But getting up that early and disturbing her could cause a scene that would wake her mother, and *she* would definitely care where Sarah was going at that hour.

She set the alarm, but all night she kept looking at her watch, wanting to catch it before it beeped. Finally, at four-thirty, she turned off the alarm, crept down the ladder, and took her clothes into the bathroom to get dressed. She wrote a note that said she was meeting Jake and Robbie and they were going to see the sunrise, which was totally true. They *were* going to see the sunrise.

She hadn't planned to include Conrad on this trip, but he started high-volume whining, so she grabbed a banana and a bottle of water—it was way too early to eat—and she and Conrad headed out.

Jake lived around the cove. She could cut through the woods to get there.

It wasn't night-time dark, Sarah almost didn't need her flashlight. It was that bleak time before the sun came up. But the air was still chilled. There was a mist on the water and the ground was damp with dew. She had that sick feeling in her stomach that comes from not enough sleep. Maybe this wasn't such a good idea after all.

Jake was waiting at the end of his dock. The lake was still, no sounds of boats or birds or distant voices.

"How come you brought Conrad?" Jake whispered.

"He wouldn't stop whining. I was going to get caught," she whispered back.

"Well you'd better keep him quiet from now on."

Conrad sat on the dock, looking totally innocent. Suddenly he stood up and gave a small whimper. Robbie's canoe came out of the mist like some mythical monster. He was at the dock before they saw him. Conrad jumped in first, then Jake and Sarah got in and grabbed the paddles, and they silently re-entered the mist. Nobody said a word—sound carries over the water. There shouldn't have been anyone else up at that hour, but they weren't taking any chances.

Sarah's sweatshirt was damp from the muggy air and she was cold. But once they caught sight of the island she felt herself getting excited. With the mist, the treetops seemed to rise out of nothing, making it more mysterious than ever.

They paddled to a small cove that Jake knew about and let the boat drift onto the shore. They weren't even going to have to step into the water and deal with bloodsuckers.

Then they pushed the boat behind some rocks, which were behind a no-trespassing sign. They didn't think it would be seen by any fishing boats. The mist hadn't lifted yet, but it was getting lighter, a gray overcast kind of light.

This was turning out to be easier than they had expected, and doing something forbidden was always interesting.

"I bet this place is loaded with poison ivy," Sarah said. She wished she had worn long pants. Sarah always said she could get poison ivy by remote control, causing her to turn into a swollen monster. "One of you two go first and tell me when you step in it."

"Not me," said Jake quickly. "This place is spooky." They were all looking at the thick tangle of weeds that began a few feet from the water.

"Come on, you wimps," said Rob heading into the brush. Sarah realized this was the first time he'd spoken. She supposed she owed him an apology. It wasn't his fault her dad talked to him. But she didn't want to think about that right now. Instead she just fell in line behind him.

The woods seemed to close in on them immediately. There was nothing that could be called a path. Branches and thorns tore at them. Rob pushed them out of his way, Sarah grabbed them from him and held them until Jake could grab them from her. Conrad managed to go around everything, still staying close to Sarah's heels.

It was murky, the trees filtered what little light there was. Sarah stepped carefully in Rob's footprints. The island was silent. There was no breeze and the dense growth captured the heat and humidity. She hadn't dried off because the mist was still making the air damp, only now she added sweat to the mix.

They seemed to be trudging upward, Sarah could feel it in her calves. Everything was dense and thick, green and wet. It was hard to tell if they were making any progress.

"How will we find our way back?" she asked. They hadn't passed anything resembling a landmark.

"We just need to head toward the water. We can circle the island. It's big, but not that big," Rob called over his shoulder.

"Let's stop and rest," Sarah suggested a few minutes later.

"You don't want to sit down, there's a lot of poison ivy here," said Rob. He was tired too, but he wasn't about to admit it.

"So, we've seen the island. It's a bunch of trees," Jake's voice was whiny. "Let's turn around."

"What about the hotel?" Sarah asked. This was turning out to be a dud and it had been her idea.

"That burned down a long time ago," said Jake.

Sarah and Rob both stopped and turned to look at him. "It did?" Sarah asked. "How do you know?"

"Everyone knows that," he said. "Where have you two been?"

"When? When did it burn down?" Sarah asked.

"How would I know?" said Jake, "but some people were burned to death, I know that. And there was something funny about the whole thing. Like arson or something. My grandfather told me about it. But we can't ask him what happened, he died this winter."

"I didn't know that," Sarah wanted to say something like *I'm sorry* or one of those platitudes that were set up for moments like this. But she hated phony phrases. She *was* sorry for Jake. He had been really close to his grandfather. She tried to think up something to say on her own, but couldn't. Another awkward moment in her awkward-moment life. "He was a nice man," she said after too long a pause.

"Yeah, he was," agreed Rob, giving a grateful glance to Sarah. He, too, had been trying to come up with something.

"Let's go a little farther," Sarah said. "Let's at least see the ruins."

They continued to trudge.

"So, you're talking to me now?" Rob asked at one point, turning around to look at Sarah. "I'm allowed to talk back?" He smiled at her.

Sarah was embarrassed about yesterday. She'd hoped he wouldn't mention it.

"Just walk," she said.

And suddenly they came to a clearing. It was the top of the hill they had been climbing. The remains of the hotel were right in front of them, a couple of chimneys, some steps, and a foundation. Beyond that were two outbuildings still standing.

They walked across the foundation. The fire must have been allowed to burn itself out. Nothing was left.

"Why didn't those buildings burn?" Jake asked, looking at the small huts.

"Maybe they weren't here then," Rob suggested.

"They're made of stone. They wouldn't burn very well," said Sarah.

"Yeah, you're right, Rob agreed. "I bet nobody's been here since the fire."

"Jake says the older kids come here. He can see the island from his place and at night he sometimes sees lights."

Rob looked at Jake, who immediately said, "It's true. I *have* seen lights."

"And you know it's the older kids, how?"

"Who else would it be?"

"Talk about how rumors get started," said Rob. He was already walking toward the nearest building.

What, Sarah wondered, was that all about? Rob was defending the older kids all of a sudden? Sarah had thrown out that idea, that he join them, because she was angry. But maybe he was really thinking about it. So he gets a growth spurt and he's ready to desert them?

The door of the first small shed was half open. Old boats, falling apart, were stacked there, long with fishing poles, boat gear, and an old generator. Everything was rotted or rusted, and the place smelled of decay and mildew. Cobwebs were everywhere, along with animal droppings.

Sarah took one look and turned away, so she was the first one to approach the second shed. This door was closed. She tried to push it open, but it wouldn't budge. There were, however, two windows. She stood on her tiptoes and looked inside. The boys crowded their heads next to hers.

There was a camp bed, all made up, a table, a chair, a shelf with books, a camp stove, and a butane tank. No cobwebs here.

"Someone's been using this," Sarah said. "Recently."

"This might explain the lights you saw," said Rob to Jake.

"I saw a bonfire. I think it was a bonfire."

"So this guy could have a fire if he wanted one," said Rob. "What else is he going to do, sitting out here by himself?"

"That's the question. What is he doing here?" Sarah asked.

"Maybe he's a watchman or something," said Rob.

"Why, exactly, would you need a watchman on a deserted island?" Sarah wanted to know.

"Why do you need all the no-trespassing signs?" asked Jake. "Are they afraid someone is going to steal their poison ivy?"

Suddenly Sarah stopped and turned around. "So where is he, this guy who lives here?" They stood in the clearing with the woods all around them, woods that must have been creeping up on this meadow since the hotel burned, inching closer and closer. Sarah could almost feel the trees closing in on them right now. Someone could be watching them from the woods. They could be anywhere, in any direction. Sarah turned in a complete circle, feeling eyes watching her.

"Let's get out of here," said Jake. He was looking all around too.

"If we're caught on the island, they'll make us leave. It's not like trespassing is a serious go-to-jail crime. We're kids. We've come to look. Big deal," said Rob.

"Fine. Let's get out of here anyway," insisted Jake. "I'm getting hungry and this has been a real bust."

"At least we know what the island is like." Sarah was feeling the need to defend her idea of coming here in the first place.

"Yeah, it's got trees," said Jake.

"I've got some power bars in the canoe," Rob said. "But Sarah's right, now we know what the island is all about."

Sarah knew she should apologize to Rob. She appreciated his defense, but anything she said now would sound moronic. She just let it go. And he had called her Sarah again, not Ramsey. She really liked the way he said her name.

"Where's Conrad?" she asked, looking around. He had been right on her heels since they landed. Now he was nowhere in sight.

She called to him and a small bark answered her from the other side of the ruins, but he didn't reappear. That was unusual. He always came running when his name was called.

She walked back to the foundation. There was a cleared patch of ground on the other side of it that had probably been a garden. Conrad was nosing around a small mound.

"Come on, boy," she commanded. He ignored her.

"Conrad Ramsey. Come here," she yelled in her most authoritative voice. He continued to snuffle in the dirt.

Sarah walked quickly toward him, scolding him with every step. Then she stopped suddenly. He picked up his head and in his mouth was a bone. It was a very long bone.

A huge chill went all over her.

"Oh my God," she gasped.

"What's the matter?" asked Rob from across the ruins.

"You'd better come here." Her voice was shaky.

They all stood and looked down at the ground in front of them. There was no doubt in any of their minds what they were looking at. The skeleton was pretty much intact, except for the thigh bone, which was still in Conrad's mouth.

Sarah couldn't take her eyes away from the horror.

"Oh God." Rob took a step backward.

"Gross," Jake muttered, turning away.

"Maybe there's a reason for the no-trespassing signs after all," said Rob, quietly.

"What do we do?" Sarah asked.

"We've got to report it to the police," said Rob.

"We can't do that. My parents will kill me for being here," protested Jake.

"Maybe there was a graveyard here," Rob suggested. "We could find out."

"But it's such a shallow grave," Sarah said. "It's no six-feet-under."

"Yeah, actually it doesn't look legal," Rob agreed. "And there's no coffin. If it were a regular burial, there'd be a coffin."

Sarah couldn't turn away from the thing in front of her. There was a dark place in her brain that carried thoughts she didn't want to dwell on. These bones had once been a human being. They would all end up like this. Just bones. So what was the point of anything? She tried to close off that part of her brain, but it wasn't working.

And then the questions—who was it? Man or woman? Young or old? Good person or bad? What was it doing here?

"There's no hurry to tell anyone," Jake said. "These bones have been here for awhile."

"That's for sure," Sarah agreed. "It takes time to become just bones, over a year at least. But there's a lot of factors, the soil, the climate, lots of things. These bones could have been here for a very long time."

Jake gave her a look. "You know all about bones, too?" he asked.

She shrugged. She didn't want to go into the science club thing.

"Unless it was someone who was burned in the fire. Then he'd be just bones, wouldn't he?" Jake continued.

"If someone had been burned in the fire, he'd have been buried in a real grave," said Rob.

"But maybe he caught on fire and he ran and then he fell down dead and all kinds of stuff piled up on top of him and nobody every found him and here he is," said Jake, pleased with his scenario.

"Or maybe not," said Rob.

Sarah looked at Jake. Sometimes he was like a little kid, without a filter between his brain and his mouth. Whatever he was thinking popped right out. So they often dismissed what he said. But every once in awhile he would come up with something important, and it was easy to miss. Sarah tried to picture a burning man, running, trying to escape the flames, falling, and the debris and ash from the fire covering him. She supposed it was possible. But then she said, "I don't think he'd be so put together like he is."

The boys agreed.

The mist had risen, but Sarah was still sweating. That didn't stop her shivering. She couldn't continue to look at the thing and she couldn't turn away.

"So how come the man who lives in the hut didn't find this?" she wondered aloud. Again she looked toward the woods. "Or maybe he did."

"Yeah, maybe he's the one who put him here, you ever think of that?" asked Jake. His voice was a little too high.

"This thing's all together." Sarah was still staring at the skeleton. "No animals have gotten to it. So it hasn't been exposed like this for very long. This was a pretty bad winter for storms. Look at all the trees and branches that are down. I think between the storms and Conrad, this thing just got uncovered."

"So we're... the first?" Jake started and then stopped.

"We really should tell the police," said Rob. "Somebody must be missing."

"Years ago, maybe. I haven't heard of anyone missing lately," Sarah said.

"Let's go. Let's get out of here," Jake urged. "We can think about it later."

"Yeah. This guy isn't going anywhere," Sarah said.

"Should we do something? Cover him back up?" Jake asked.

"No. We can't touch anything. We'll have to tell somebody. Maybe not right this minute, but we'll have to. And they need to see it just like we're seeing it," insisted Rob.

"But now the animals will get to him," Sarah pointed out.

"You're right, we can't wait too long to tell somebody," said Rob.

Jake was already walking back the way they had come. Sarah was about to follow when she realized Conrad still had the bone in his mouth.

"Drop it," she commanded.

Conrad didn't immediately obey. He obviously didn't want to give up his treasure. Rob grabbed the bone from him and threw it back into the grave. Sarah took Conrad's collar and dragged him with her for a few feet. Once into the woods, she followed Rob and Jake followed her, exactly as they had come.

Either they hadn't made a path on the way there, or they were in a totally different place. They were going downhill and so it should have been easier, but by now they were all spooked. The woods seemed menacing. Someone lived on the island and there were bones on the island. They didn't know if the two things were connected; they didn't know anything.

The woods seemed darker. It should have been brighter without the mist.

They trudged forward for what seemed like a long time, longer than coming up the hill.

"Hey–look over there," called out Jake.

They stopped. He pointed off to their right.

It wasn't a clearing, it wasn't even a path in the normal sense of a well-trod line. But there was definitely something, the weeds and growth trampled down, the branches pushed aside.

"Let's take it," Jake urged.

"Should we?" Sarah asked cautiously. She was still seeing eyes watching her. "Wouldn't it be Island Guy's path? I have no desire to meet him."

"So? He tells us to leave," said Jake.

"And if he's the cause of the bones? Wouldn't he be a bit concerned about us snooping around?" Sarah asked him.

"Look, we've been walking a long time, way too long. We're probably going around in circles," said Jake.

"I think that's exactly what we're doing," said Rob. "This is taking us way too long."

The boys didn't wait for Sarah's consent. They both started walking toward the path.

"I want to get off this creepy island as fast as I can." said Jake. "I hate it here."

Sarah followed them. Now she was in the rear, those watching eyes were now directly on her back. She kept looking around. Even Conrad seemed nervous, or was that only her imagination? Maybe he was just aware of how uptight she was.

The island was silent. There were the natural background sounds, insect buzz, bird calls, things not usually noticed. But the three of them were the only ones to occasionally make a real noise, like snapping a stick, or tripping over a log.

So, when the sound came, it seemed all the more startling. It came from somewhere in front of them, a definite crash. They all stopped; Sarah actually collided with Jake.

"Watch it," he whispered.

"Probably just a branch falling," said Rob. But he, too, was whispering.

"There's no wind or anything," Sarah observed.

"Let's turn around," said Jake.

"We don't want to go back, we need to get to the beach," said Rob.

"Send Conrad," suggested Jake. "Tell him to go ahead of us."

"And what's he supposed to do? Come back and give a report?" Sarah asked.

Conrad acknowledged his name with a whimper. He knew when he was being talked about, and he always assumed it was a compliment. Not a bad way to live, Sarah had often thought. But if he were to meet up with the island man, he wouldn't necessarily warn them. Until proven otherwise, the man would be greeted as another best friend.

As they continued, the walking became easier. The path was wider and the foliage not as dense.

The woods came to an abrupt end at the rocky shoreline. The day had cleared and the water was sparkling. The sudden brightness, after all the shady trees, took a minute to get used to.

"This isn't where we landed," said Jake, looking around.

"I think we're way east of there," said Rob. "What time is it?" He pointed to Sarah's watch.

It seemed to her that they had been on the island forever. Yet her watch read 7:30. She couldn't believe it.

"And the sun is over there," Rob pointed. "So we are on the east side of the island and we landed on the north side. We need to head..." Suddenly he stopped. "Look," he said.

There, about sixty yards down the rocky beach, was a boat, tied to a tree. This was no rotted derelict that had been abandoned years ago, it was a small rowboat, like a million other rowboats, but in good condition. It was turned upside down and there was water still glistening on the hull.

"The island man," Jake and Sarah said in unison.

"He's here. And he must have just left the beach," said Rob in a hushed voice.

"So why didn't we run into him?" Sarah asked.

"Maybe we did. Maybe he just saw us first," said Jake.

"Maybe that's what we heard back there," added Rob.

They all turned and looked toward the woods. Was he watching them right this minute? They didn't speak again. They turned and started running down the beach, climbing over the rocks and washed-up debris. Sarah kept looking back at the woods. She could almost feel him.

They were all winded when Rob finally slowed down and started walking. They were stumbling over everything by then. There was no question of talking; they didn't have any breath left. Sarah's side ached and her legs felt rubbery. Still they walked. There was a good reason this was called the Big Island—it was endless. Sarah could hear Jake gasping for breath behind her.

At one point, she tripped over a log and Rob grabbed her arm before she hit the ground. It was an effortless gesture on his part, just one hand held out, steadying her. But as he held on, until she regained her feet, she was very aware of his touch and the quick smile he gave her. She was having very different feelings about Rob than she ever had about Robbie. She wasn't sure that was a good thing. They trudged on.

Rocks look like rocks, water looks like water. They could pass their boat and not realize it. They had, after all, taken pains to hide it.

They were sure they had walked right past it a long time ago when Conrad started barking and Rob came to a halt. He didn't speak, just pointed, and there was their boat peeping out from behind the rocks and the no-trespassing sign. Conrad kept barking and running around it.

None of them could say out loud the "Thank God" they were all thinking. All they could do was take a minute to stand there and pant and try to get up enough energy to lift the canoe and get it into the water. It seemed an insurmountable task, although it was something they did all the time.

They hauled it out of its hiding place and pushed it until it floated. Conrad was panting as much as the rest of them, but he managed to jump eagerly into the boat.

They could barely climb in, let alone lift a paddle.

It was a feeble crew that maneuvered the canoe across the lake on the way home. Again they didn't speak, but this time it was because of exhaustion, not because they didn't want to be heard.

Rob pulled up at Sarah's dock first.

"We've got a lot we need to talk about," he said before pulling away.

"Yeah, we do," she agreed.

"This afternoon. Let's meet at our place. We'll talk about it then," he suggested.

"Fine. But not until about three o'clock. I'm going back to bed," said Jake.

"See you at three." Rob waved and started to paddle away. Then he stopped and looked back at Sarah.

"It's a good thing you're speaking to me again," he said with a smile. "It will make our conversation a lot easier."

4

When they were little kids, Sarah and the boys had called the big hill behind Sarah's cottage a mountain, and really believed it was. Now they knew better, but it still wasn't an easy climb. Sarah was panting when she got to the top. She stopped for a minute to catch her breath. One side of the hill had been ripped apart by the big machines that had dredged out sand for beaches on lakes that did not naturally have beaches. The top of the hill had once been the place of mock wars and pirate games. She smiled to herself, remembering all the hours they had had spent up here.

There was the only tree on the hill, a huge oak that may well have been there since even before the loons. They had built a pathetic tree house up there, just a few boards nailed together. They seldom climbed up anymore, but when they were younger, they called it their secret place. There was nothing secret about it. It was in plain sight of everything and everybody, except that most people never bothered to climb the hill. This was one way to get to the Beach Club from their side of the lake, but the older kids drove there now and everyone else seemed to go by boat.

The boys were leaning against the tree. Sarah sat down facing them.

"So, it wasn't just a bad dream, huh?" she asked.

"No, I'm afraid not," Rob said, as he held out a bag of chips to her. "We've got to tell somebody about the bones."

"We'll be in trouble for trespassing and it's none of our business, and since when have you become such a Boy Scout?" Jake's voice was peeved.

"I'm not a Boy Scout," Rob spit out, too loud, too angry.

"Whoa. What's that all about?" asked Jake. "What's the big deal?"

"Just don't call me that, I don't like it."

Both Sarah and Jake stared at him, open-eyed.

"Over-reaction, huh?" Rob said, realizing how he must have sounded.

"It's not like it's the biggest insult in the world," said Sarah.

"But it is to me. I was called that once before and it's still gnawing at me."

"What happened?" asked Sarah.

He paused, trying to decide whether or not to go into it. Then he shrugged.

"Like, right before I left the city, there was this party. Ashley Thompson's parents were out of town, and everyone showed up at her house. They found some beer and got into the liquor cabinet and all of a sudden they were wrecking the furniture and Ashley was crying, not just crying, hysterical, so I tried to stop them. These were my friends and they were acting like idiots. I got mad, I mean really mad, I was ready to fight. The first thing they called me was a Boy Scout, then it got a lot more foul-mouthed than that. Anyway, I was standing there with my fists ready, probably looking like a total dork, but I was freaked. I knew I was about to be beaten bloody. I wasn't even shouting back. And they backed off. I don't know why, but they did. So that made me a Boy Scout and not in a good way. What would you have done?"

"That took a lot of guts," Sarah told him.

"Yeah. I couldn't have done that," admitted Jake.

"You'd have let them tear up the place?" Rob asked him.

"I don't know. But just me by myself? I don't know. I mean, you're right, they would have beaten you to a pulp."

Jake gave Sarah a sidelong glance, as though afraid of her disapproval.

"Some of them are still mad at me," Rob said. "I'm hoping they'll forget it over the summer. What about you, Ramsey? You wouldn't care what people called you, would you?"

"Sure I'd care. What? I don't have feelings?"

"That kind of stuff just doesn't seem to matter to you. I wish it didn't matter to me."

"Maybe I'm just used to people calling me names. I've grown up on my sister's insults. Anyway, calling somebody a Boy Scout is no big deal. And what you did was a good thing. So, if we call you a hero, does that make up for it?"

"No. That's embarrassing. That's not why I told you the story."

"We know that. We'll never call you a Boy Scout again. We promise, don't we, Jake?"

Jake grinned. "No Boy Scout, no hero, no nothing."

Sarah decided it was time to change the subject. "So, what are we going to do about the bones?"

"Seems like you're the deciding vote," Rob told her.

"Easy for you to say, Rearden, my parents will kill me for going to the Big Island. Worse, they'll take away my new kayak. That was the big threat when I got it. Straighten up or no kayak."

"Straighten up?" asked Sarah, interested. "What have you been up to?"

"Absolutely nothing. My parents don't have a clue. I'm disgustingly boring. They don't like my hair, my clothes are too baggy, they don't like my friends. If only they knew what some of the kids in my school were doing."

"Yeah," agreed Rob.

Sarah laughed. "Yeah," she said. "I get the 'why aren't you friends with that nice Carter boy?' That nice Carter boy happens to be the biggest scum bag in the school. You're right, parents don't have a clue."

"Okay, here's what I think," said Rob. "We found a body. You can't just ignore that. It's like a misdemeanor to trespass, but it's like a crime not to report finding a body."

"A body? We haven't called it a body before," said Sarah. "That makes it like it's a murder or something. And it's probably just old bones."

"Yeah," said Jake. "Like you said before, it's maybe like a graveyard or something."

"No. Ramsey was right. That was no grave. It was too shallow," said Rob. "And remember, no coffin."

"So maybe there was like a farm on that island a long time ago," said Jake. "People who lived off by themselves had to bury their own dead."

"There'd still be a coffin. They'd make it themselves," insisted Rob.

"So maybe those were Indian bones," suggested Jake. "I don't think they used coffins." He and Rob both turned to Sarah.

She shrugged. "I don't know how Indians buried their dead. I don't even know which tribes were around here."

"I thought you knew everything," said Jake, genuinely disappointed. Rob was a little surprised too. Sarah usually did know that stuff.

"Wait a minute," said Sarah suddenly. "We don't have to tell anybody. If the bones were just exposed by Conrad, then the island guy will see them. Let him tell the police."

"Unless he has something to do with the bones," Rob said.

"But like we said, they could be old bones, probably are. He's living there now. Nothing says he was living there when the bones were buried," Sarah insisted.

"Okay," Rob agreed reluctantly. It seemed like a simple solution, and that's what they were all looking for, a simple solution, but it didn't feel right. "We still should find out who he is and why he's there."

"No. We should forget the whole thing. The guy will tell the police. It will be in their hands and I won't get in any trouble and me and my kayak will live happily ever after," said Jake. He stood up. Problem solved.

Rob knew it was a cop-out, but he didn't feel like arguing any more. "Okay," he said. "I'm not a big fan of trouble. He can tell the police. Just so they know." He stood up as well.

Sarah just nodded her agreement and followed them across the hill.

"How about we slide down?" said Jake. "We haven't done that in years."

"We don't have anything to slide on," Sarah said.

"You're no Jennifer Lopez, but you do have a butt," Jake answered.

"And new shorts," she told him. "You can take out the seat of your pants if you want to. I'm walking down."

Rob laughed. He and Jake both had on jeans.

"Wuss," he said to her, knowing it would goad her into going. Maybe it was the idea of sliding down or maybe it was the fact that they had postponed getting themselves in trouble, but he felt suddenly more like his old self.

Jake went first, shouting all the way as he gained momentum. Rob and Sarah took off at about the same time. She was laughing, he was holding his breath.

It only lasted a minute. At the bottom, they both spotted Jake trying to pull up his pants. His parents might have had a good point about his baggy clothes. Sarah wasn't the one with the sorest backside. Both she and Rob got into a laughing fit that they couldn't stop. It felt good. For the moment, none of them were thinking about the bones.

5

The discovery of a skeleton should not have gone unnoticed. It should have rippled around the lake like a tsunami. Yet three days went by and nobody had said a word. Sarah, Rob, and Jake went down to the Beach Club every day just to hear the gossip—nothing.

The local paper came out on Wednesday. The three of them decided to paddle across the lake to the general store at about noon, when they were sure the copies would have been delivered.

Plenty of copies, but no news of anyone telling the police about the bones.

On the way back they went by the island, slowly circling it, looking for the man's boat. Maybe he had been away. Maybe he hadn't taken the time to walk around the foundation and hadn't discovered the thing.

The boat was exactly where they had seen it before.

"Sometimes people don't notice things in their own backyards," said Sarah. "Maybe he just hasn't stumbled on it yet. Maybe he'll find it tomorrow or the next day."

"We can't wait much longer," Rob argued. "We owe it to the dead guy, don't we?"

"We don't owe anything to any dead guy," Jake said. "We didn't put him there. He's probably been there for a gazillion years, anyway. Maybe he's prehistoric."

"Not quite prehistoric," Sarah told him. "And if he were, archaeologists would still want to know about him."

It was easy to keep putting off making a decision.

But then something else happened that took their minds off the bones temporarily.

It was Saturday morning. Sarah's mother greeted her at breakfast, all excited, with that phony enthusiasm she could project.

"Oh Sarah, I have news," she said. Sarah's first thought was that her father was coming up after all. Her next thought was that her mother had heard about the bones, but that didn't exactly make sense. Her excitement wasn't that kind of excitement.

"You are going to be so pleased," Sarah's mother said.

Sarah would be pleased if she'd just spit it out. Her mother could take ten minutes to open a Christmas package. She loved to drag things out. Sarah had no patience with it. It drove her insane.

"Finally, you might actually get to have a friend," Jennifer told her.

"I have plenty of friends," Sarah argued, still having no idea of what this was about. And she did have plenty of friends. She was just not willing to turn herself into an android to join a group. And besides, she truly believed that the quality of a few friends was far more important than the quantity of a whole bunch.

She turned to her mother. "Please, just tell me."

"The Carson cottage, it's been rented for the summer. A family named Fraser. And they have twin girls just your age. Isn't that wonderful?"

"I guess so," Sarah said. She had been perfectly content with her summer friends and this was yet another change. "I guess so," she repeated.

"You should go right over this minute and introduce yourself," said her mother.

"Can I get dressed first? And I'd kind of like some breakfast." Sarah wasn't really trying to be sarcastic, at least she didn't think she was.

"They're cute," said Jennifer. "The question is, will they want you as a friend?"

Sarah knew that there was no point in talking back to her sister. They only voice that penetrated Jennifer's brain was her own.

She got up and poured herself a bowl of cereal. Did they want her to just barge in there and say, "Will you be my friends?"

"Maybe I'll get Rob and Jake to go with me," she said. "We can all be friendly."

"I guess that would be all right. But these might turn out to be special girl friends for you. You might not want the boys there," cautioned her mother.

"We're all going to meet each other sooner or later," Sarah insisted.

"She's afraid to go by herself," said Jennifer. "Do you want me to hold your hand?"

"God forbid." Sarah gulped the rest of her cereal and got up to get dressed.

The Carsons were an older couple. They hadn't been coming up to the lake much the last few summers. Their cottage was two doors down from Sarah's. But it's not like in the city, two doors down—there were woods in between. From the water, it seemed close; from the land it could be a hike.

Sarah got in her canoe and picked Jake up first. He wasn't any happier about doing the introducing thing than she was, but Mrs. Hawkins, Jake's mom, thought it was a wonderful idea.

"I saw the girls in the store," she said, waving them off. "They're adorable."

After they picked up Rob, Jake said to both of them, "Let's get this over with and go sailing. This is the first windy day."

The Hawkins had a lightning-class boat at the Beach Club. Later on the races would begin. Jake, Rob, and Sarah had only won one of them. They had beaten Tommy Emmerson, maybe the most irritating guy in the older kids' group. That had happened the last race of the season last summer. They figured they'd do really well this year.

When they pulled up at the Carson dock, they were all reluctant to get out.

"This is so dumb," Sarah complained.

"It was your idea," said Jake.

"It was my mother's idea." They started walking slowly up to the house.

This cottage, like all the cottages, had a big screened-in porch across the front. Porches weren't locked. Actually, cottages weren't locked during the summer. You were expected to go through the porch and knock on the door beyond it, except those doors were usually wide open to catch the breeze, as was this one. Sarah opened the screen door and was headed toward the inner door with Jake and Rob right behind her, when a voice from the corner stopped them.

"Omigod, what do we have here?"

They all turned. Sarah happened to be looking at Jake and saw his mouth fall open. It stayed that way. People should realize how ridiculous they look with their mouths open.

There was a blonde, long-legged, living, breathing Barbie doll rising from the sofa. She did some sort of gesture with her head that made her perfect hair sway around her face. It was long, straight hair that looked too smooth to be real. She was model-thin and in her hand she held a bottle of red nail polish. She had one foot to go. She smiled, her gaze aimed laser-sharp toward Rob. Sarah felt invisible.

The girl waited a moment, but nobody spoke.

"My name is Megan," she said. She hesitated. "And you are?" She was still looking only at Rob.

He turned on his super smile. "Rob." he sputtered. "Rob Rearden. Nice to meet you." He nervously shifted his weight.

Jake finally managed to close his mouth long enough to say, "I'm Jake."

"My name's Sarah Ramsey," Sarah said, feeling like a twit.

The girl didn't even glance at either Jake or Sarah.

"And there's two of you?" asked Rob, recovering himself with what was almost a leer.

She smiled. "Two identical. Too bad there's not two of you. Or are there?" She had a little tinkle of a laugh. It sounded well-rehearsed. "It was so nice of you to come over and introduce yourselves," she continued.

"That's the least we could do. Welcome to Loon Lake," said Rob.

Sarah gave him a look, but he didn't notice. Now he was taking credit for this stupid visit?

"Melissa, come see what I've found," Megan called out.

Melissa appeared immediately and she was, indeed, a duplicate copy of her sister, except that she had already finished her toes.

They both had on very short white shorts with the same pink halter tops. Sarah imagined they wore a lot of pink.

Melissa had the exact same smile as her sister. It showed way too many too-white teeth.

"Well," Sarah said, wanting more than anything to get out of there. "We just wanted to welcome you."

"Thank you," said Melissa. She, too, only looked at Rob.

"Would you like some lemonade?" Megan asked. "My mother just made some."

"No, thank you," Sarah turned to Jake. "We have to go, don't we?"

"No way, I'd love some lemonade." His mouth was open again.

"Come with me, Rob," said Megan. "You can help me carry the tray."

"Please, sit down," Melissa gestured to Sarah and Jake, as the other two left the room. She eased herself into a wicker chair, crossing her very long legs.

Sarah couldn't think of a single thing to say to this girl. "We can't stay long. We're going sailing, aren't we, Jake?" She spoke deliberately, so he'd get the hint.

"Ah, we can do that anytime, Ramsey. He was mesmerized by the girl in front of him. "In fact," he added, speaking to Melissa, "you could come too."

"Your boat can't hold all of us," Sarah pointed out.

Jake looked at Sarah and frowned. She immediately knew who wouldn't be included.

"Do you sail? Sarah asked Melissa.

"Omigod, no. All that wind blowing every which way. I don't quite see the point." She ran a hand through her hair.

They sat in uncomfortable silence for a few minutes until Megan and Rob returned. He was carrying a big tray with glasses and a pitcher and a plate of cookies on it.

Once Rob was back in the room, Jake and Sarah became invisible again. Sarah was getting really annoyed with this situation.

She took a cookie. Homemade oatmeal raisin, her favorite. The twins watched her eat it and then they each took a cookie, gave it one small nibble, and put it down. Sarah was in no way fat, but she wasn't anorexic either. The way the twins were looking at her, she felt fat. The boys finished off the plate.

"What in the world is there to do around here?" Megan asked.

"Everything," said Jake with enthusiasm. He told them about the boat races, the Beach Club, the canals, and the river rafting, and he didn't even notice that they were barely listening.

"I mean, what do you do for fun?" asked Melissa. "Aren't there any parties?"

"The older kids have a lot of parties," Rob said and proceeded to give a testimonial of the very people they usually mocked.

"But they don't include us," Sarah quickly added. "We're not old enough for them, you two are fourteen, aren't you?"

"We are. But I met a boy at the mailboxes yesterday. Tom Emmerson, I think his name was. Do you know him?" asked Megan.

"Yeah. We beat him in a sailing race," said Jake with pride.

"Well, he didn't seem to think we were too young," said Megan. She smiled at Rob.

Sarah knew she needed to get out of there. She stood up. "Thanks for the lemonade. It was nice to meet you." She started walking toward the door, expecting the boys to follow her, but they didn't.

So what? It was her canoe. They could find their own way home. But it was a lonely walk to the dock and she paddled back to her place way too quickly. Anger is a good fuel source. Her mother would be asking her why she hadn't stayed longer, so she took a trip around the lake. It always soothed Sarah to paddle a canoe. But the lake would have had to become a small sea to give her enough room to soothe herself at that point. She kept seeing the way the twins had looked at Rob, so adoringly. And he was eating it up. She thought he had more sense than that.

She had to pass the Big Island coming and going. It was still and dense and mysterious looking. She didn't see the island man's boat this time. Maybe he was finally talking to the police.

Her canoe had a small leak and with all her paddling, it was taking on too much water. She finally had to head for home.

6

Later that afternoon, Rob saw Sarah on the end of her dock.

"Ramsey, how rude can you be?" he yelled at her as he glided up in his canoe. "That was really nice, drink their lemonade and then split. And really considerate, leaving Hawkins and me to walk home."

"Your choice," said Sarah. She didn't feel even a bit bad about leaving the twins and wasn't about to apologize for it. "But listen, I went by the Big Island and the man's boat wasn't there. So maybe he's finally telling the police."

"Or maybe not. He's got to leave pretty often to get supplies." Rob reached out and grabbed her dock with one hand.

Sarah looked at him, noticing that he was already getting a tan, his hair was lighter, and his eyes looked really blue. She could see what the twins saw. She shouldn't be mad about that, but she could be mad about Rob's reaction to them.

"So how come, if he leaves the island, we've never seen him?" Sarah asked, trying not to sound angry. Why should she care if he got all goofy over those two blonde stilts?

"What makes you think we haven't? We don't know what he looks like. We wouldn't know him if we did see him," he said.

Sarah thought about that. It was true. "But we know everyone around here. You hardly ever see a stranger."

"Sure, you do, Ramsey. You just don't pay attention. People come to fish and everyone around here has house guests sooner or later. We don't know everyone. Besides, it could be someone we do know, ever think of that?" He let go of the dock and used his paddle to keep the boat close.

"I don't know anyone who would live on an island."

"Sarah, you don't know what you know. Half the people around the lake are just people you see. You wouldn't know if one of them decided to live out there."

This time, she didn't like the way he had said "Sarah."

"If someone had a perfectly good cottage, they wouldn't go off and live on an island," she shot back.

"People do all kinds of strange things," he told her. He let his boat drift a little.

Sarah didn't know why she felt compelled to argue with everything Rob said. She couldn't help herself. She was mad at him and with the twins and with her dad and with the lake in general.

"We need to tell the police," he said after a minute of silence. "We really can't wait much longer."

"You keep saying that, but maybe it's just none of our business. We don't want to get Jake in trouble, do we? Actually, we'll all be in trouble, I just don't have a kayak to lose."

"There's right and there's wrong," said Rob, knowing as he said it that he was doing the Boy Scout bit again. "This might be a crime. It's a crime to cover up a crime." He gave another swipe of his paddle, getting closer to the raft again.

Sarah had to think that one over. Was just pretending you never saw something a crime? She didn't think so. And besides, he was using his superior voice again.

"So let's go back and see what's happened," she said, and was sorry the minute the words came out of her mouth. She didn't want to go back to the island. She didn't want to see those bones again.

"Why?" asked Rob.

The trouble was now she was stuck with herself, stuck with her own words.

"To see if the island man covered up the grave," she said. "If he did, then we should go to the police because he obviously knows about the dead body and he didn't do anything about it. That would mean he's involved, wouldn't it?"

"And if he didn't?"

"Then he hasn't seen them yet," said Sarah. "We could wait some more, but we'd know more than we do now."

Rob was quiet for a moment, considering it. He tried to picture the grave, to picture somebody just covering it again with dirt. Would they do that?

"Okay," he said. "Let's go back and look."

They made a plan for the next morning. They decided not to include Jake. Sarah said she didn't think he'd go again anyway. He was too worried about his kayak.

But later that night, Rob called and canceled. He said he couldn't do it the next morning. The twins wanted to go to the Beach Club and he had promised to take them over in his boat. What, Sarah wondered, was that all about? He was at their beck and call? It was a good thing for him that he told her over the phone. She wanted to smack him.

But then he blew her off again the morning after that. She didn't even listen to his excuse. She just said "Fine," and hung up. She knew her anger was getting her into trouble. She hadn't wanted to go to the Big Island at all. Now she was suddenly possessed with going. She'd go by herself. She'd get this whole thing over with. Who needed Rob Rearden anyway?

It wasn't quite as early this time when she and Conrad slipped out of the house, but no one else was up. She left a note that just said she was taking the motor boat. She was glad it was a rowboat with a motor, that made it easy for her to row away from the cottage. She used the motor once she was in the middle of the lake and rowed again as she approached the island.

The man's boat wasn't there, so she felt fairly safe. But the motor boat was heavier than Rob's canoe. She couldn't drag it up the beach and hide it as they had done before. So she just pulled it up onto the shore in the same little cove they had used the first time. She could only hope that the big rocks out in front would keep anyone from noticing the boat. She intended to be quick about this and would be gone before most people were out on the water.

That meant she had to hurry. They hadn't made a path, but she let Conrad lead and he seemed to know where he was going. Dogs were wonderful that way. They could smell a million more scents than humans. When they smelled spaghetti, they smelled each ingredient–tomatoes, oregano, hamburger. Now, as they walked, Conrad must be smelling each of them. A little Jake here, a bit of Rob over there and, of course, herself. He had his nose to the ground and he kept going uphill, so she just followed behind him.

It wasn't misty today; it didn't seem to take her long at all. They arrived at the ruins before she was even anticipating it.

The clearing was in bright sunlight. It didn't seem so threatening. But she stopped and held Conrad's collar and listened. The man could be anywhere watching her. He could have come from his side of the island as she was coming from hers. Or he could have put his boat in a different place she didn't know about.

But there was only silence. His shack was closed up, as it had been before. Still, she walked slowly past the burned hotel, looking all around, pausing and listening.

Then she walked directly to the bones. She didn't have any time to waste. Once again she was on top of the grave before she saw it. Everything was the same. The bones were exposed. The man just hadn't seen them yet. So they wouldn't have to go to the police right away. They could avoid getting in trouble for a little bit longer.

Conrad leaned down and once again grabbed the thigh bone in his mouth. She guessed he had some sort of claim on it. But it was gross, seeing it hanging out of his jaws. However, it gave her an idea, so she let him have it for a minute.

Just as she had before, she stood and stared at the skeleton. It was hard to believe it was real. There was such a Halloween feel to it. Maybe it wasn't real, maybe this was all some kind of sick joke.

She made herself stand still and look, notice, note. In science club they were taught to observe. Step back out of themselves and look for details. This time she could do that. First of all, this grave had been here for awhile. A small tree had formed roots in the grave itself. That meant some time had passed. There was dirt still covering most of the bones, but she could see what was there. And now she noticed something else. There were wisps of clothing here and there, something black or that had turned black. The bones were large. She made a guess that it had been a man. There were buttons and a zipper and shoes that had survived the years. There were bits of some shiny silky fabric, and then something else. Both arms were crossed on the chest and underneath the left arm was something dark and hard to identify. It was bigger yet thinner than a wallet, but still she thought it might be leather. It was covered with a mossy, mildewed film.

She leaned down and tried to pry it away without actually touching the bones. It was a rectangular shape, about ten inches long and six inches wide, with a snap and button closure. She managed to slide it part way out from the hand bones that rested directly on it. The snap had rusted away and she was able to ease open a corner. Inside was something yellowed with age. Paper—she could see that it would shred at the merest touch. It was an envelope. She needed to leave. She needed to get out of there, but her curiosity was in high gear.

Finally she stood up. She motioned Conrad to follow her, which he did, with the bone still dangling out of one side of his mouth. She led the dog up to the man's shack.

"Drop it," she commanded Conrad.

He looked at her with great disappointment. Did she really mean it? She would take away his prize?

"Drop it," she repeated.

Conrad was such a good dog. He did as she commanded and she gave him a pat on his head and all was forgiven.

She intended to walk away after that, intended to hurry back to the boat. The man would see the bone and would get curious enough to look around. He would find the grave and all their troubles would be over.

But that curiosity bug had bitten her: she returned to the bones. Once more she leaned over and tried to grasp the leather case. If Rob had been here this never would have happened. He would be giving her a lecture on disturbing evidence.

As she knelt there, she suddenly had a picture in her mind. She could see it clearly, a man in a suit, his inside jacket pocket would be right there where the hand was, and the leather case had been in the pocket. The silky stuff was the pocket lining.

She tried to ease the case out from beneath the hand. It moved a little. But as she tugged very gently, the bones moved with it. Then Conrad gave a little bark and she jerked at the sound and the case was free. She held it in her hand. It was covered with all kinds of stains. She hated even to think what body fluids had contributed to those blotches. She could imagine blood and dissolving body tissue and all the consequences of putrefaction.

She tried to pull at the envelope, but it crumbled at her slight touch. Carefully, she eased it out, leaving little pieces of it on the inside of the case. She managed to open it, shredding and tearing it more, even though she was trying so hard to be careful. There was one sheet of paper. It too shredded at the merest touch. Little flecks fell into the grave. There were smudges and blotches on the paper. She could only read a few words, and it had been a full page of writing. The signature on the bottom was two words. She could make out what was probably the third or fourth letter of the first name, 'e.' Then it disappeared into a blur. The next word was gone except for an 'a,' at least she thought it was an 'a.'

The other words in the letter itself, that she could read were, "intimidation," "police," "welcome," and one word that was the most clear of all, "caveat."

Only four words, but she felt a terrible chill. If she had more time, she might decipher more, but just then Conrad let out another bark. This time he didn't stop. Conrad didn't bark at nothing. She quickly tried to stuff the paper back into the crumbling envelope, it disintegrated even more. It was almost impossible to get it into the case. Then she thought about fingerprints. They would test it for fingerprints, wouldn't they?

She tried to use her shirt to wipe off where she had touched the leather, but she couldn't wipe the paper, it would shred to pieces. She placed the case back where she had found it.

Now she heard what Conrad had heard. There was a sound coming from the brush behind the two small shacks.

She shot to her feet and dashed toward the woods.

"You, stop," called a deep voice. She ran as fast as she could and Conrad was in full gallop. They pounded through the underbrush. No reason to try to be quiet now. But he was coming behind them, making even more noise than they were. Conrad was now in front. His tail was wagging. He thought this was some kind of a game. But he was running full-out and Sarah was right behind him.

Her breath now came in gasps. They still had a long way to go. She wanted to hide someplace, maybe climb a tree. Then she would be able to see who he was and maybe he wouldn't spot her. But there wasn't time and Conrad didn't climb trees. They just kept running. The man sounded closer.

She could hardly breathe at all. Her legs were aching. They were going downhill and she was losing traction. She kept slipping and sliding. She couldn't afford to fall, he'd catch them for sure.

She could see a brightness in front of her. The beach. Thank God. But now what? She had to push the boat out into the water. All he had to do was keep running. She could almost feel his hand on her shoulder.

She reached the beach and dashed toward the boat. There was a crash behind her. She didn't dare take the time to turn around. She seemed to have gained some super-human strength. She had heard that fear could do that. She shoved the boat and a few seconds later it started to float and she gave it a mighty extra push just as Conrad jumped in. Then she jumped in herself. The boat had some momentum from the shove and was in deep enough water to start the motor in just another few seconds.

But, of course, it didn't start, not on that first pull. And she pulled three more times after that and it still wouldn't start. Then she took a deep breath and pulled again. The sound of the motor catching was the most beautiful thing she had heard in her life.

Now she took time to look back at the island. There was no one on the beach. He must have fallen down as she had almost done so many times.

She wished he hadn't. She wished she could get a look at him. But she had escaped and that was enough to ask for at the moment. Her adrenaline was in full-flight mode. She was practically jumping out of her skin. She couldn't rev the boat to go fast enough. Still she was panting and trying to catch her breath, as was Conrad. She had never heard him pant that hard, and he hadn't had fear to contend with.

Sarah had a pretty good imagination and it worked in pictures. Maybe everyone's did or maybe some people thought in words. Anyway, with her, it was pictures. If she heard a voice or imagined something, she saw it, clear as a movie. When she thought about something or someone, she saw them. It wasn't always accurate. One time her mother was working with a woman on a committee and Sarah kept answering the phone when she called. Just from her voice Sarah had a picture of her in her mind. She envisioned her as one of those pigeon-like women whose bosom precedes her into a room. But, when she finally met the lady, she was small and frail and kind of cute. So much for her imagination. Still, she couldn't turn it off, it was the way her brain worked. And the island man with the big voice, she saw him in her mind. He was huge and hairy and evil looking. He was nightmare quality. She really wanted to turn off that particular picture.

She wasn't ready to go home. She was too agitated. She pulled along side Jake's dock. He saw her from his porch and came sauntering out. She almost left, his frown was that evident.

"So what's the matter with you?" she asked.

"They left without me," he said, in a dejected voice as he reached her boat.

"Who left where?"

"Rob and the twins. They went without me."

She did almost pull away then. She was so sick of the twins. But he climbed into her boat and sat in the middle seat and stretched over and to give Conrad a pat.

"Exactly where did they go?" she asked, spacing her words carefully.

"We were going to show them the canals."

That almost did it. The canals were their territory. From way back, they were their territory. When they were younger, they had caught turtles and painted their backs and then re-caught the same turtles the next year. They had watched tadpoles grow into frogs. They had played hide and seek, each in their own canoe. It was easy to disappear among the rushes and cattails and feel like you were in another world.

"Thanks a lot for including me," Sarah said.

"We didn't think you wanted to be with the Fraser twins," he answered.

"That part's true," she admitted. "So how come they left without you?"

"My mom made me do some stuff and they didn't even wait. I'm really ticked off. Rob sure is acting weird."

"Yeah," she said and they let a little silence happen. She had a moment of feeling better with Jake. The enemy of my enemy is my friend. She knew the twins couldn't care less about him, but he was too dumb to realize that. He was in the same boat as she was, literally and figuratively, even if he didn't know it.

"Well, let me tell you what I just did." Sarah described what had happened to her on the island. He did that opened-mouth thing again and he didn't say a word until she finished.

"Geez, you went there by yourself? And you touched the bones? Creepy." He sounded impressed.

"Yeah, but the letter, what do you think it meant? I mean I think it proves that there's been a crime committed. It was some kind of a threat or something."

"You couldn't read much," he said, but he was obviously thinking about it.

"I wish I'd had more time. But when the island man yelled at me I was really scared."

"So what's he look like?" He leaned forward eagerly.

"I didn't see him, I just ran. But he's big and tall. I know he is just by the sound of his voice."

"You should have looked back," he said.

"Yeah, I'm sure you would have stopped and stared. Which would have been pretty dumb under the circumstances."

"I guess this means we've got to go to the police." He didn't look happy about his suggestion.

"What about your kayak?"

"Actually, I've hardly been in it. We've been doing stuff with the twins and it's a one-man kayak. So they take it away from me for awhile. I guess it's not so important."

The twins again.

"I've gotta go," she said trying not to sound angry. She motioned for him to get out of her boat. He jumped onto the dock.

"They really are kind of nice," he said.

"Fine." She gave the rope a pull. Again nothing happened. She wanted a dramatic exit. This motor didn't cooperate with her moods.

"Want me to help?" he asked.

"No." Her voice came out more angry than she had intended. She gave another pull and roared away.

So now what? She still didn't want to go home and explain where she had been, and yet she was freaked-out with where she had been. They did need to go to the police. Or should they give the man one more day? He'd see the thigh bone. He'd have to wonder about that. It should make him look around. And, besides, it was a difficult thing to purposely bring trouble on yourself.

She cruised around the lake, trying to figure things out, trying to get herself calm. It wasn't until she saw Rob's big green canoe across the water that she made the turn toward her own dock. She had no desire to meet up with him and his new girlfriends.

7

The next day Sarah sat on her porch reading a book. She loved to read, and it was a pretty good book, but her mind kept wandering. She knew she had to make a decision and soon. Jennifer was lying out on the raft with her three of her friends, and her mom had gone to lunch with some of the other mothers. They did that a lot because the dads weren't around during the week. Quite a few mothers on the lake were teachers, including Sarah's mom. They would never admit it had anything to do with the summers off. So Sarah was alone with her thoughts and her worries and was beginning to realize that Jennifer might be right. Maybe she didn't have enough friends. Being alone because you want to be is one thing. Being alone because nobody wants to be with you is something else altogether. And the boys were sure keeping themselves busy.

Her mother didn't get back until after four o'clock. That's a pretty long lunch. But she came out onto the porch with a big smile on her face, which made Sarah realize how little she smiled anymore and made her feel guilty about not spending more time with her, actually talking to her. Sarah knew she wasn't the only one suffering from this dad thing.

"You look like you had a good time," said Sarah.

"Oh, I did," said her mother, still smiling. "I was introduced to the twins' mother, Beverly Fraser, today. She's a very nice person. She wants to meet you. She said she was sorry she missed you when you went over there. She did say she met the boys and wondered why you left so soon."

She paused, but just for a minute, Sarah didn't even have time to start coming up with an excuse before she went on.

"She was telling us something quite intriguing. We were all busy welcoming her to the lake, but it seems she has a very old history with Loon Lake. Her family had a cottage here for years until her parents sold it. Actually, her great-grandfather owned the Big Island and the hotel that used to be there. At some point it burned down and he was killed in the fire. None of us had any idea of their connection to the lake. It's interesting, isn't it?"

Sarah sat up straighter; this actually *was* interesting.

"Do they still own the island?" she asked.

"They're not really sure. It's been tied up in legal problems for years. There was a partner involved with the hotel and there's always been a question about who owned the land.

"Was Mrs. Fraser's great-grandfather buried on the island?" Sarah asked eagerly.

Her mother looked at her oddly. "I wouldn't think so," she said. "Several people died in the fire. I'm sure they were all buried elsewhere."

"But all these years later—why have they kept it posted?"

"I don't know. You could ask Mrs. Fraser or ask the twins. What pretty girls they are. I saw pictures of them. You should make more of an effort to get to know them. Robbie and Jake have been showing them around, but their mother was hoping they'd meet some nice girls up here. She says they're too interested in boys at home and that's one reason she decided to spend the summer back at her old lake."

"Yeah. They *are* too interested in boys," Sarah agreed.

"You could invite them over here. Why don't you do that? Invite them to spend the day with you tomorrow. I have their phone number."

"They wouldn't want to spend the day with me," Sarah said. "Believe me." Then she thought about it for another minute. "But you're right. I should make an effort to get to know them. I'll just go over there again. Maybe right now."

Her mother couldn't have been more pleased if Sarah had told her she'd won the Nobel Prize. She was absolutely beaming.

Sarah decided to walk over. It took longer and she needed to plan what to do and what to say. She followed the shoreline, which meant she had to take off her sneakers and walk in and out of the water and the muck among the rocks.

So she arrived with dirty feet. So what? At least she didn't get any bloodsuckers. But she hadn't come up with any brilliant ideas about how the conversation would go. She would just have to wait and see.

She also hadn't thought that Rob would be there.

She would have turned around when she saw his boat, but they were outside on the end of the dock, the three of them. The girls were in bikinis, one red, one blue. They were lying down in lounge chairs and Sarah could smell the sun block from where she was.

Rob was sitting up on the dock, his feet in the water. He watched her approach.

As soon as he saw her notice him he smiled his big smile. It's almost contagious. Her mouth muscles wanted to reply, but she wouldn't let them.

"Hi," he said.

At that the girls sat up. They didn't say anything, just watched her walk down the dock toward them.

"Hi. So how did you like the canals?" she asked the girls.

"B-o-r-i-n-g," said one of them. She didn't know which twin she was talking to, She couldn't tell them apart.

"Nothing but water and weeds," said the other.

"The most exciting thing we saw was some dumb turtle on a lily pad," said the first.

"Jake was pretty upset," Sarah told Rob. "He couldn't figure out why you didn't wait for him.

The girls glanced at each other and giggled.

"The twins were in a hurry to get there," said Rob. He laughed too. Some inside joke, Sarah guessed, resentfully.

She sat down on the dock next to Rob. The only two lounge chairs were occupied by the twins. But she turned away from him, which made her turn toward the girls.

"Want some more diet soda?" the girl in the red swimsuit asked Rob.

"Sure," he said. He held out his hand and she reached down into a cooler and brought out a can dripping with ice.

"Thanks, Megan," he said.

So red suit was Megan.

She looked at Sarah for several seconds before she offered her one too. Sarah was thirsty, but she shook her head no.

"I hear your family owned the hotel on the Big Island," Sarah said to the girls. Rob sat up and looked at her.

"They did?" he asked.

"Yes, they did," said Melissa. She was lying down, her face covered with a big hat. "Who cares?"

"I do," both Rob and Sarah spoke together.

Melissa removed the hat and looked at them.

"Why?" she asked.

Rob and Sarah glanced at each other. Sarah was trying to think of something to say and not coming up with anything.

"It's interesting," Rob said quickly. "Island lore and all that kind of stuff."

Sarah figured if she had given them an answer, they would have ignored it. Since it was Rob, they both sat up.

"Our great-great-grandfather had a hotel. It burned down. He was killed," said Megan.

"Our great-great-grandmother never recovered from it," said Melissa. "It was very sad. They must have loved each other very much."

"It really was a sweet love story," said Megan looking dreamily at Rob.

"So, he was killed in the fire?" Sarah asked.

"Of course, what else?" This was Melissa.

"When did this happen? Like what year?" asked Sarah.

"Why are you interested in this ancient history?" asked Megan in a bored voice.

"What I can't understand is why you've never been here before," Sarah said. "I mean, you must be one of the original families on the lake."

"Our family used to have a cottage here, but my grandparents sold it when my mother was a teenager," Megan said.

"Oh." Sarah couldn't identify with that at all. She could not think of anything that would ever make her leave the lake. "But your mom grew up here?" she asked.

"Oh, yes. She's crazy about the place. She's been trying to get us back here for years. My dad isn't interested in lakes or cottages. He's a golfer when he has any time at all, and he doesn't take much time off even for that. He's a doctor and he's busy."

Sarah looked toward the house. A woman in shorts and a T-shirt was pulling weeds from around the porch.

"Is that your mother?" she asked.

Both twins turned and looked.

"Yes," they said together. Their voices blended. Sarah suspected they answered together a lot.

She got up and started walking toward the cottage. This was not something that Sarah Ramsey would normally do. She wasn't somebody who chatted with other kid's parents. But she was way beyond feeling shy; she wanted information about the skeleton they had found and would do anything to get it. What she didn't realize was that Rob was right behind her. When she glanced back and saw that he was, she looked at the expressions on the twin's faces. Identical. Priceless.

So she had a smile on her face when she approached the woman.

"Mrs. Fraser?" The woman looked up from her weeding. Sarah introduced herself.

Mrs. Frazer put down her spade, took off a gardening glove, and held out her hand. Sarah always felt a little silly shaking hands, it seemed like such a dumb thing to do. But she leaned down and gripped Mrs. Fraser's hand.

"Sarah, I've been wanting to meet you. I enjoyed meeting your mother today. It's so nice that you and my girls are the same age." She had that identical beam that Sarah's mom had when the idea of friendship with the twins was mentioned. Sarah wondered if there was some kind of pact that mothers had about pushing kids together when they had nothing in common.

"My mother told me about your family, about owning the hotel on the Big Island and that you grew up summering at the lake," Sarah said. "Maybe you even knew my dad." She didn't know why she had thrown out that last bit. Just to make conversation, she supposed.

Mrs. Fraser had been kneeling and now she tried to stand up. Rob reached over and helped her to her feet.

"Some would think it's silly," she said, "weeding at a rental cottage. But I love gardening and I can't stand to see weeds take over. I was even thinking of planting some Impatiens here. Wouldn't they look pretty?"

"But your name wouldn't have been Fraser, would it?" Sarah asked, curious because Mrs. Fraser hadn't answered her question.

Mrs. Fraser was silent for a minute. Then she smiled. "No, my maiden name was Gerard. I spent every summer on the lake until I was seventeen. I loved it here. When my parents sold the cottage, I was heartbroken."

"Once you know the lake, it would be hard leaving it," Sarah said.

"It was very hard." Again she smiled. "I so hoped my girls would come to love the lake like I did. But maybe I waited too long to bring them here. They're already asking when we're going back to the city."

"Not soon, I hope," said Rob, anxiously.

"We're going to stay the summer," she said with determination. "And Rob, I appreciate you making the effort to show the girls the lake."

"No problem," he said with a grin.

"So, Mrs. Fraser, did you know my dad?" Sarah didn't know why she was pursuing this. It was not what she was here for. But Mrs. Fraser seemed to be avoiding her simple question.

There was a hesitation. Finally Mrs. Fraser said, "Yes, I knew your dad. Matt Ramsey and I were friends from when we were very small through our teens. Our cottage was just around the cove. We had wonderful summers up here." She looked at the lake with a wistful expression.

So what was so hard about that? Sarah wondered. Back to the point. "Do you know much about the hotel and how it burned?" she asked.

"My family didn't like to talk about it," she said. "It was a horrible thing. My great-grandfather was killed, you know. My great-grandmother never recovered from her grief. It was all very sad and rather a taboo subject around our house."

"And nobody lives on the island now?" Rob asked.

"No, of course not. I hear it's posted property. Supposedly my family owned the island once, but we couldn't prove it. They could never find any records."

"That's strange," said Rob.

"Not so much up here in those days. This was farm country, the hotel started out as a rustic camp. There were no real towns around here then."

"Are you going to visit the island while you're here?" Sarah asked.

She paused. "I hadn't planned to. I don't think I have anymore right to be there than anyone else."

Then she held out her hand to Sarah again. "I'd better get dinner started. It was nice to meet you. Say hello to your mother for me." She turned and went up the steps to the porch and into the house.

"She's nice," said Rob.

"Yes, she is," Sarah agreed, "But I wish she knew more about the hotel and the fire."

"You can't just bust into other people's family business," he said. "If they don't want to talk about it they don't have to. We need to go to the police and you need to stop obsessing over this whole thing."

"I know," Sarah admitted. "Tomorrow. We'll tell the police tomorrow."

She hadn't mentioned her return visit to Rob. She didn't want to see that superior look of disapproval on his face again. She had had quite enough of it lately.

8

They had made up their minds. They couldn't put it off any longer. They had to tell the police. But it's a scary thing to do, to walk into a police station, even when you're just reporting something.

This particular police station was like an afterthought to the firehouse. It was an addition at the back, behind where the fire engine was kept, very small and inconspicuous. It was in the cluster of buildings that everyone called "the Foot" because they lay just beyond the foot of the lake.

When Rob, Jake, and Sarah walked in the door, they were all nervous.

"It's the right thing to do," said Rob. "It's like our civic duty."

"They'll be pleased with us," said Sarah. "They'll thank us for letting them know about it."

"Quit trying to convince yourselves," said Jake. His eyes were wide.

They were shown into a tiny room with no windows. There were some chairs lined up against the wall. Sarah noticed a chain coming out of the wall and attached to an ankle cuff. She poked Rob and pointed it out. At that moment this whole thing became very real. And frightening. This was a mistake.

Jake had noticed it too. His eyes got wider.

Two men came into the room. They sat down behind a table in the two chairs that were placed there, facing the line-up of chairs against the wall. They motioned to the three kids to sit.

One was an older man with white hair, a big stomach and a wrinkled uniform, who told them he was Police Chief McCarry. The other one was younger, and his clothes were overly neat. There were pleats stitched into his shirt. He told them he was Officer Ellis. They talked like that, using their titles.

"So, you're here to report something?" asked Officer Ellis.

"You know, you should have your parents with you," said Police Chief McCarry.

"Just to report something?" Sarah asked.

"It's customary, but let's hear what you have," he answered.

They let Rob do the talking. But the officers kept interrupting.

"You're aware that the island is posted. You saw the no-trespassing signs," said Officer Ellis.

There was no right response to what was a statement, not a question.

"We just thought we'd pull up for a minute," said Rob. "Then we got kind of curious. It was a dumb thing to do."

It was obvious that Officer Ellis liked Rob. The chief didn't seem to like any of them. He just glared. There is a certain way some people can look and make others feel instantly guilty. The chief had that down to a science. His face was expressionless, but his eyes just stared. Sarah kept her attention on Officer Ellis.

"And why didn't you report this immediately?" Ellis asked. Rob had given them that information. Sarah hadn't planned to mention that they had waited so long. They hadn't coordinated their stories.

"We knew we'd be in trouble," Jake said. "My parents are going to kill me. They'll take away the new kayak I got for my birthday."

The chief gave an audible exhale.

"But our consciences got the better of us," Rob said and then looked a bit sheepish. He was well aware of how phony that sounded.

The chief gave another exhale before the he finally added something to the conversation.

"Tell me more about the man living on the island," he said. He looked at each one of them in turn.

"We didn't actually see him, just his shack. But it sure looked like someone was living there," Sarah said.

Jake gave her a look. She hadn't said anything about her return visit to the island to the police, so she could hardly start describing him chasing her. After all, she hadn't seen him then either. And she didn't want to mention the letter or say that she had touched evidence. And this was hardly the time to let Rob in on that information. The police could find the letter for themselves.

"We thought maybe it was a watchman or someone like that who was living in the shack," Jake said. "Is there a watchman on the Big Island?"

These people didn't answer questions. They only asked them. And they were big on repetition. The kids had to tell the story several times.

Sarah didn't know when she started to feel her hands begin to shake. It came over her gradually. She folded her arms to keep anyone from noticing. This was taking too long and she didn't want to be here anymore. And now it appeared that everything they had done was wrong and maybe criminal. Going to the island had been her idea. She was responsible for all this trouble.

Finally, after they had described the whole thing once more, they were told to go home. The chief said they'd investigate. They were told not to go anywhere.

"If you have anything to add, let us know. And bring your parents next time," the chief said as they walked out.

They paddled back to their side of the lake in Rob's canoe. None of them spoke. The police were one thing. Now they had to tell their parents.

As it turned out, Jake's parents were the least upset. He had to confront both of them because his dad was there as well. But they didn't even mention taking away his kayak. They thought he had done the right thing by telling the police. Rob's mother, on the other hand, was very disappointed in him. She does disappointment really well. Both Sarah and Jake felt sorry for the guy.

Sarah's mother's reaction was by far the worst. She started crying, and that was so odd. Sarah had seldom seen her mother cry.

"Oh Sarah, what were you thinking? Why would you not tell us? Why would you sneak off to that island? Why would you get involved with a dead body? I can't deal with this right now." There were tears streaming down her face. She ran into her bedroom and closed the door. Sarah could hear her crying in there and she felt like a piece of dirt. She knew her mother was upset about Sarah's dad. She knew her mom had looked sad, but she hadn't cried before, and Sarah was now the cause of it. She didn't think she would have cried if she hadn't already been feeling terrible. That's what made it so upsetting. Punishment would have been easy, but there was no punishment. There was only that closed door and the muffled sobs.

Jennifer, of course, was much more vocal. By late afternoon the news was all around the lake. Bones had been discovered on the Big Island. Sarah, Rob and Jake were involved.

"What a mess you've made of everything," Jennifer told Sarah more than once. She had suddenly become her mother's protector. Sarah's sister, who had been giving her mother a bad time for the last year, was in there rubbing her back and commiserating with her about Sarah's foul deeds.

Finally, Sarah had to leave the house. She took the motor boat to the Big Island, but it was now surrounded by a flotilla of idling boats of all descriptions. The police hadn't exactly circled the place in yellow tape or anything, but there were a couple of what the kids called the Water Pigs in boats waving everyone off. These people were more used to checking life jackets and fishing licenses. This was a big deal for them.

Sarah did notice that the island man's boat was nowhere to be seen.

The people she knew in the other boats pointed her out and then stared at her. She couldn't take that for long. She went back home.

After that came the worst thing of all. They didn't hear anything.

There were, of course, wild rumors. The fact that the three of them had made the discovery implicated them in some way. Sarah never heard anything specific, just the idea of being involved seemed to tarnish them. And the fact that they hadn't reported it immediately made them look guilty of something. Nobody seemed concerned that they had trespassed.

Even Jennifer's friends suddenly started to talk to them. Sarah appreciated that the invisible status she had always had seemed to disappear. But it was like the older kids had turned into policemen and asked accusatory questions, or else they wanted gory details. Except of course for Rachel Young, she didn't ask questions; instead, she was sympathetic.

"You're really brave, Sarah," she told her. "I would have so freaked out. Bones. Ugh. The guys in the white coats would have had to come to the island and take me from there."

And Rob and Jake were hanging out with Sarah again. They were kind of stuck with each other, so they spent a lot of time up on the top of the hill by their pathetic tree house just reading magazines and playing cards. They didn't even talk very much. But they had always been okay with silence between them.

The Frasers became the most interesting people on the lake because of their connection with the island. The police had been over there several times and suddenly the lake people started including them in everything, even Jennifer's friends, who now invited Megan and Melissa to sit with them in their selected spot at the Beach Club.

Sarah, Rob, and Jake knew this because they were back to juvenile spying. They'd leave their tree and walk the hill and peer down at the club and watch. They had no desire to join the people having such a good time down there, they just watched, feeling like the outcasts they were.

One good thing did happen as the result of the discovery. Sarah had heard her mother on the phone with her father. She had stopped crying, but she wasn't initiating any conversations with Sarah. She'd call her to dinner, or tell her to turn her light out at night, and that was the extent of their communication.

But her mom and dad were on the phone every night for the three nights following the visit to the police. She heard her mother tell him the story. After that there was more listening than talking. The next night he called and again, it was mostly listening, or her mother's voice would be so low Sarah couldn't make out the words from her bedroom. The following night they talked for almost an hour. Sarah fell asleep listening to her mother's whispering voice.

Then it was Friday evening and suddenly he was there. Sarah's dad was banging his way through the back door of the cottage, carrying his suitcase and a couple of boxes of things they had forgotten.

Sarah was in full motion, running toward him before she stopped suddenly, unsure of herself. But he held out his arms and she ran into them full force. He felt so good and solid and there. Nothing bad could happen now. Sarah didn't cry, anymore than her mother did. But at that moment the flood gates opened and she was definitely crying. It was all mixed up—happy, sad, guilty, everything.

"It's okay," he said in that comforting voice that had always reassured her. And it was. She stopped crying. She let go and looked at his face.

He smiled at her. He had dropped his suitcase and the boxes, and he led her over to the sofa by the fireplace and sat down beside her.

"It seems like there's been a bunch of excitement up here," he said.

There was still a hiccup in Sarah's voice. "We shouldn't have trespassed."

"You shouldn't have had to see what you saw. Are you okay?"

Nobody else had asked her that question. No, she wasn't okay.

"I keep seeing those eye-sockets," she said and realized how many times she had pictured that skull and those missing eyes.

He gave her an additional hug. "Poor baby," he said.

"Are you here to defend me? Have I done something really wrong? We did trespass."

"That's barely a misdemeanor. Don't worry about it. Don't do it again, but don't worry about it. The police might have pursued it before they had a murder investigation to worry about. But believe me, it's a non-issue now."

"A murder investigation? We thought about that, but not in a real-life kind of way."

"It's in the police report. The city papers will have it tomorrow. The man had been shot."

"Wow," she said, then realized how inappropriate that sounded.

"So in a way you've done them a favor, exposing a crime, but what I can't understand is why you delayed telling the police. You know better than that. Robbie certainly knows better than that." That did it. Her anger at her father came right back.

"Is it true? Do you talk to Rob about your cases?"

"Rob?"

"He used to be Robbie," Sarah said. "Now he's all full of himself and he's Rob. He's like all grown up."

"Not so much that he didn't go trespassing with you," Dad noted.

"So, do you?" she asked. "You never discuss your cases with me." But he had pulled away from her. She looked up. Her mother was coming through the doorway.

They both stopped. The atmosphere in the room was total tension. Sarah watched her parents' faces, but they didn't tell her anything. They were staring at each other, waiting for some move or sign or something.

Sarah knew when she wasn't wanted. She got up and went outside. For once she didn't even want to overhear what was being said. She knew it wasn't any of her business. Not that anything like that had bothered her in the past, but this time, she couldn't handle it. She did, however, have her fingers crossed. Conrad was right at her heels. He could smell tension. He didn't like it either.

She sat in the canoe. It was tied to the dock and she made no attempt to go anyplace. She just sat and looked at the water. This early in the season the sun would remain up for several more hours. But there was the feeling of dusk, no breeze, a stillness to the water, a quiet around the lake, a softening of the sun.

This was the time she liked best to be out in a canoe by herself and she usually didn't want to go home until the sun set. The whole lake would turn pink and glow with a radiant calm. It was a wonderful feeling of being alone and yet being a part of the lake and of the world.

But tonight she didn't want to go out on the lake, even if the canoe hadn't been leaking this year. She wanted to be here to talk to her dad. She would just have to wait.

She stayed there for a long time. The rosy glow had started when she heard her dad call her from the cottage.

At first her mother sat in the room, but after a few minutes she got up and went outside. Her turn to sit looking at the water. Jennifer, of course, was no where to be seen. So it was just Sarah and her dad. And he was the opposite of her mother—he got right to the point.

"I called and talked to the police. We're going back there tomorrow," he said.

"They want to see me again? We already told them about finding the bones."

"The usual procedure is to question people more than once."

"Why? We weren't lying."

"They don't think you were lying. But people leave things out. Did you leave anything out?"

There it was. She wasn't ready to answer that question. So she went back to the question her dad hadn't answered.

"First, you tell me. Did you discuss your cases with Rob?"

He smiled and gave her a hug.

"Guilty as charged," he said. "But it wasn't anything you would have been interested in. He wanted to know all about habeas corpus, extenuating circumstances, and burden of proof, terms he had heard on TV and didn't totally understand. You got any terms you want explained?"

She would have loved to have come up with one, but she couldn't.

"I was pretty impressed that he was thinking so seriously about his future," her dad said. "That's not a bad thing."

Up until very recently Sarah hadn't given any thought at all to her future. She hadn't progressed much from ballerina, doctor, or astronaut type of thinking. Now, with the science club and forensics, she had glimmer of the direction she wanted to go. But she wasn't ready to talk about it. She wasn't ready to be teased about an idea that was too new and too fragile. She could just imagine what Jennifer would do with a gem like that. But she wished she had said something to her dad. She wished he knew she had some serious thoughts about her future.

"So, now your turn," he said. "Was there anything you didn't tell the police?"

You can't distract a good lawyer and Sarah could never get away with fudging the truth with her dad.

"I went back to the island again. I didn't tell them that," she said.

"Why? Never mind that now. What happened the second time?"

"I did a bad thing. I touched the evidence. I knew better, but I did it."

"Explain," he said. He didn't sound angry, so she told him about the letter, and about the man chasing her.

He listened intently. He was very good at listening. In fact, Sarah realized that you don't notice how few people actually listen until you talked to somebody like her dad.

"That was very dangerous," he said when she had finished. "You need to think about that. Some strange man chasing you? And you put yourself into that situation. That isn't good."

"Yeah, but about the letter. What do you suppose it means?"

"Hard to tell from the little you could read. It might not have any connection at all. Things usually don't fit neatly together, not in real life."

"So I should tell the police about my second visit?"

"You, Sarah, my pet, know the answer to that. The truth is always best and withholding something is as good as a lie."

He gave her an additional hug and got up. "Enough for now. We visit the police at nine-thirty tomorrow morning. Maybe we'll find out more then."

"Are you going to defend me? For trespassing?" she asked. She was perfectly serious.

"I'm here as your parent. You don't need a lawyer." He walked outside; she supposed it was to talk some more with her mother. She hoped that was a good thing.

That night Sarah went to sleep in a nanosecond. A great big boulder had been lifted off her shoulders.

9

So once again Sarah had to visit the Loon Lake back-door police station.

Matt Fraser stormed in there like a one-man invading army. This was a side of him Sarah had never seen. He had definitely put on his lawyer hat.

"What were you thinking?" he said as soon as Chief McCarry identified himself. "You interviewed three kids without any parents present?"

"I mentioned it to them," he said. "As they told me, they were simply reporting something they had seen."

"So there was no interrogation?" Dad asked.

"No. Absolutely not." The chief gave Sarah one of his looks. Did he practice being scary in front of a mirror? But maybe it was in the eye of the beholder. Her dad didn't seem to notice.

Finally they all sat down in the same little room Sarah had been in before, and her dad became instantly more friendly. It was like he had established something and now could just be himself.

"This has been quite an ordeal for the kids," he said. "It was a terrible thing for them to see."

"I agree," said the chief. This was a different man than Sarah had seen before. He didn't glare a bit at her father.

"So, what's going on with the case?" Matt Ramsey asked. "I read a report that said it was a homicide."

"That's right," said the chief. "He was shot in the chest."

"And lab reports? How old are the bones?" Sarah's father had a professional tone in his voice.

"No definite date. The state lab is handling it. But we got a guess of somewhere between fifty and seventy years. We'll know more when we get the final report."

"What about the letter? Could you make it out?"

The chief sat up. "What letter?"

"My daughter admitted to me that she went back to the island. She saw a letter among the bones. I'm afraid she tried to read it."

The chief stood up. "What are you talking about? We didn't find any letter." There was no doubt about his glare now.

"But it was there," Sarah insisted. "It was hard to read. It was in an envelope inside a leather case, and it was falling apart. It was right where a man's inside jacket pocket would have been." Her voice was shaky. "And that second time the guy who lived in the shed chased me. I didn't see him. I never saw his face or anything. He just shouted at me and started chasing me."

"And why wouldn't you have mentioned this before?" asked Chief McCarry. He spoke slowly, the way adults do when they are very angry.

How could Sarah explain that she hadn't told Rob yet and therefore didn't want to tell the police? Talk about sounding stupid.

"Obviously," said her father, "she was upset. Sometimes you don't think of everything when you're upset. She's only fourteen."

Sarah figured the chief would have been screaming at her about then if her dad hadn't been there. He was red in the face and he looked like he was holding his breath. Maybe counting to ten?

"My daughter knows she did something wrong. She had touched the letter. After thinking about it, she knew that was a bad thing. It's a natural reaction to try to avoid trouble, and she's here now trying to make that right."

The chief continued to glare at Sarah. He asked her to describe the letter, and she did. She repeated the four words she could read.

"But I may be wrong about the words," she told him desperately. "They were really hard to read. The ink was all brown and most of it was faded away and there were stains and I was trying not to tear the paper."

Chief McCarry kept them there another half hour. He still liked repetition. But he wasn't that comfortable talking to a lawyer. He finally let them go.

They walked out of the building, and Sarah breathed a big sigh of relief.

"Your part's over now," said her dad. "Don't worry about this anymore. Let them handle it."

"But what happened to the letter?" she asked. "Somebody took it. I did see it."

"I believe you, so somebody must have taken it. But it's not our concern anymore."

"It must have been the island man. He took it. That's why he didn't report the bones."

"Not our concern," her dad repeated.

She was silent for a minute. "Dad, I almost forgot. You knew Mrs. Fraser. Well, you knew her as Beverly Gerard, I guess."

He stopped walking. He smiled. "Sure, I knew Beverly Gerard. We were really good friends growing up. Why?"

"She's back. She has twin girls and they're renting the Carson cottage. But did you know that her great-grandfather owned the island hotel? Did you know all about the fire and everything?"

"She's back at the lake? That's something. And she has twins?" He had a strange look on his face.

"Did you know about it—the fire and all?" Sarah repeated.

"That I did. We were fascinated about it for awhile, just like you. Beverly hated that her family wouldn't tell her any of the juicy details."

"Do you think the bones are related to the fire?" she asked.

"Sarah," he said, "I think you've indulged in way too much TV and mystery novels. It's none of our concern. And only during the forty-five minutes of a TV show is everything on the scene related. But I'll admit something to you, just so you won't feel so bad. Beverly Gerard and I trespassed on the

Big Island, just like you did. I think all the kids do it sooner or later. Anyway, we were looking for something too, some marvelous clue about the fire, except we didn't find anything. And I wish you hadn't found anything either. But now you need to drop it and forget about it."

Sarah didn't argue. He had come up here for her. He had protected her at the police station; she was grateful. But the idea of forgetting about this whole thing was ridiculous. He had always told her that curiosity was a good thing. She agreed. But she didn't remind him of that. They drove home and she went along with his small-talk.

He was only up for the weekend, so he made things happen quickly. The Frasers were invited to dinner that night. All of them. Sarah's mom had to rush out to the store and Sarah was forced to clean the cottage. Her phantom sister, of course, was not home, and her dad was busy working on the boat motor. Sarah had told him how hard it was to start this year. He promised to patch the leaky canoe as well, and clamp the raft.

At first Sarah was resentful about the cleaning, but as she gave the rooms a quick sweep, she began to see the whole evening as being to her advantage. Maybe her dad and Mrs. Fraser would start remembering their interest in the hotel and the fire. There might be things they knew and just weren't telling her. If she could get them talking, who knew what might come out? Her dad was so eager to see his old friend that he might not notice her pushing the conversation where she wanted it to go. Or at least that was her plan.

The Frasers arrived precisely ten minutes late. The girls were dressed in cute little sun dresses. Perhaps they hadn't learned yet that nothing was dressy around the lake. Their mother, however, was with the program. She had on khakis and a T-shirt.

It was kind of fun for Sarah to see her dad and his old friend, Beverly, greet each other. There was an awkward second or so. It must have been one of the first such moments her dad had ever experienced. Awkward didn't enter his world.

Then he gave Mrs. Fraser a quick peck on the check and the moment was over. They took up where they had left off years ago, jabbering away. Sarah's mother was busy in the kitchen and except for Dad keeping her wine glass filled, she had little to do with the conversation. They covered all the years since Beverly Fraser had left the lake.

Jennifer came in at the last minute with her "I'm so rushed because I'm so popular" look. She went over to the twins and greeted them like she would greet her own friends, which really broiled Sarah's insides. How come she was a juvenile nuisance and they were all buddy-buddy?

Her mom had made lasagna, which was one of her specialties. Sarah had been delighted when she had heard that. The twins would hate it. They would consider the smell alone fattening.

But that evening was due to be one of many surprises, and the fact that the twins dug into the lasagna was only the first.

"This is delicious," enthused Megan.

"Yes, Mrs. Ramsey, this is wonderful," said Melissa. "I've never tasted anything so good."

Beverly Fraser could roll her eyes almost as well as Jennifer. "When they go out, they pretend that they actually eat," she said.

But the twins had won Sarah's mother over completely.

Sarah had a whole strategy planned, about bringing up the subject of the hotel fire. But the second surprise was that she didn't need it. Mrs. Fraser had brought several bits of news.

The first was that her husband would be arriving that week for a brief visit.

The second was who he was bringing with him.

"My grandmother is coming up," Mrs. Fraser said. "Do you remember her, Matt?"

"Of course I remember your grandmother. A nice lady. Backed us up and kept us out of trouble a couple of times, if I recall." They smiled at each other.

"When she heard about the discovery on the Big Island, she insisted on coming," Mrs. Fraser said. "She hasn't been well, this is quite a trip for her."

"We can't believe it," said Melissa. "Nana hardly goes out of the house. And now she's totally freaked on coming up here."

"My dad tried to talk her out of it, but she is *so* not listening," said Megan.

"She really is determined," said Mrs. Fraser. "It's such an about-face. Nana would never even tolerate a question about the island or the fire. And now this. But she never stopped talking about the lake."

"Well, It will be delightful to meet her," said Sarah's mom.

"What about your parents? Have they ever been back?" Matt Ramsey asked.

"No," said Mrs. Fraser. "I think they feel terrible about selling the cottage. They needed money at that point in their lives. But I know they've been sorry they had to do it. They've moved to Florida, so they're around water all the time now. We hardly ever see them. I know Nana was upset when they sold. I don't think she's ever forgiven them."

Melissa turned to Jennifer. "Nana would tell us stories about the lake when we were little," she said. "But we were always warned never to mention the words fire and island in the same sentence."

"She watched her own mother grieve for all those years," said Mrs. Fraser.

"Was your grandmother there? Was she on the island when the hotel burned?" Sarah asked.

"Oh, no," said Mrs. Fraser. "She was only seven years old then. She would hardly have remembered. It was just that her mother was so terribly upset."

"When was the fire?" Sarah asked. "When did it happen?" She hoped she didn't sound too eager.

"Sarah," said her mother. "Perhaps Mrs. Fraser doesn't want to talk about that."

But Mrs. Fraser continued. "The hotel burned down in 1930," she said. "It's a year my family won't ever forget, although I don't think anyone but my great-grandfather ever spent much time at the hotel. It was a business, and the family had the cottage. But the fire was a terrible thing. Three people were killed. As I said, we were never encouraged to discuss it."

"But those people—they were all buried somewhere else?" Sarah asked. "One of them wouldn't have been the skeleton we found?"

"Sarah, enough," said her mother sharply.

Mrs. Fraser saved her by changing the subject.

"I really can't believe you're an attorney, Matt. You always said you'd never follow in your father's footsteps. You said it was way too boring."

Matt Ramsey had the grace to smile. "I'm a criminal attorney. It's anything but boring."

"And he hardly ever discusses his cases," Sarah blurted out.

"What do you mean hardly ever?" said Jennifer. "Don't you mean never?"

"Only to Rob Rearden," Sarah said. "They discuss his cases."

Jennifer looked at her dad, as surprised as Sarah had been.

"Rob is so cute," said Melissa.

"But not as cute as Tommy Emmerson," said Megan. "He's hot."

Sarah was still looking at Jennifer. Jennifer was not pleased with that remark.

There was nowhere to go but downhill from there. Jennifer was not subtle. She turned away from Megan and started talking to Melissa about how cute Rob was and how age-appropriate he was for her.

Megan kept trying to re-enter the conversation.

"I heard that the cutest one is Rob's brother, Kyle," she said. "But I've never seen him."

"And you probably won't see him this summer. He's in college now, just finished his freshman year," said Jennifer pensively. "He's jot a job in the city so he's not life-guarding at the club anymore. And you're right. He's gorgeous."

"He makes Tommy Emmerson look like the dork he is," Sarah added, as much just to say something as anything.

The adults in the room had not been fascinated with this conversation. They were talking among themselves. At least Matt Ramsey and Beverly Fraser were talking. They were reminiscing about those years on the lake when they were kids. Jean Ramsey was watching and listening to them.

The conversation never came back to the skeleton or the Big Island.

10

The next day was the first sailing race of the summer. Loon Lake had sailboat races, not regattas. Everything was low-key. But that didn't mean the races weren't important. Everyone on the lake took an interest in them. There were no fancy timed races, just a starting line, a mark to go around and a finishing line. And over the years the people had formed their own rules.

Jake, Rob, and Sarah were a pretty good crew; they understood each other. They didn't have to shout and yell like some in the other boats. The couple of times they had managed to get in a practice this year, it seemed that was still true, but they hadn't done enough practicing and Sarah and Rob were concerned. Jake wasn't. On the way to the club, as they walked over the hill, Jake was freaking out with excitement.

"I bet we win every race this summer," he said.

"That's not going to happen. We have to be realistic," said Rob. "We need to concentrate on one race at a time."

"There's absolutely no reason we can't win every one," insisted Jake.

"So let's set our sights high," Sarah suggested. "Can't hurt."

There was a big crowd at the Beach Club and a lot of excitement in the air.

The races started with the smallest boats, like the sunfish, and worked up. Not that there were any big boats on the lake. Jake's boat, the *Wind Rider,* was a lightning, and the lightning class race was second to last, which left a lot of time to get nervous.

The day was sunny but a little chilly. There was a breeze, not a great one, but enough. When they got in Jake's boat and approached the starting line, they maneuvered into a good position. The race-committee boat was a rowboat with one person in it. He waved his orange flag, and they were off. Jake was at the tiller. This was the windward leg. Rob was handling the mainsail and Sarah had the jib sheet. Sometimes it was a fight, heading into the wind, but not today.

The sun was in their faces, the water dashed by, and they could feel the wind power. Jake was tacking beautifully. Sarah often teased Jake about being like a swan, awkward on land, but great at the tiller, where he came into his own, like he was one with the boat.

They started off in the lead, and were just thinking they had it made, when suddenly another boat pulled up beside them. At first they just noticed three guys, then they saw that it was the *Enterprise,* Tommy Emmerson's boat. They couldn't miss his ever-present friend, Hulk Norton, who was, indeed, a hulk. Tommy and his crew won more races than anyone on the lake, but Jake, Rob, and Sarah had beaten the *Enterprise* once last year. It freaked Tommy out just because they were younger. Tommy kept changing his third crew member. He yelled a lot.

"Come on," Sarah shouted. "They're gaining on us."

They were approaching the halfway mark. Rob got ready to help swing the boom and ease the mainsail. Sarah was ready to let out the jib.

They were neck-and-neck with Tommy's boat. Then they got a gust of wind and Jake sailed close to the mark, almost clipping it. The boat was heeling way over to the side. Jake held the tiller and they jibbed around the mark.

Now it would be a downhill run to the finish line, the wind behind them.

Tommy was on the port tack. Boats on the starboard tack have the right of way. But Tommy's boat was dangerously close, looking ready to ram them. The overtaking boat is supposed to keep clear, and you're supposed to disqualify yourself if you break a rule. Nobody on the *Wind Rider* trusted Tommy with any of that. Everyone on Tommy's boat was yelling.

Jake looked desperate. They had all wanted to win this first race so much. The two boats, still neck-and-neck, had left the others behind.

It was still close as the *Wind Rider* reached the finish line, but their bow was in front. The horn sounded, the flag waved. They had won.

It took several minutes for their hearts to stop racing. Everyone was shouting and yelling at them and clapping. It was a great feeling, especially right now, after feeling like pariahs for a week.

Later, in front of the club building, sodas and iced tea and cookies were being served, Tommy Emmerson walked toward Sarah. She couldn't imagine what he wanted and that made her a little wary.

"Nice race," he said.

"Thanks, but you need to tell Jake and Rob. They did it."

"Maybe, but I'd rather tell you. You're prettier."

That stunned her. What was she supposed to say to that? She didn't do compliments well; she had no idea how to handle them. She mumbled a thank you and reached for a cookie she didn't even want.

"You'd be really pretty if you'd fix yourself up a bit," he continued.

"Thanks a lot." She could do sarcasm, that was no problem for her.

Sarah hadn't ever really looked at Tommy Emmerson before. But after the discussion at dinner last night, she scrutinized him. Megan and Jennifer both thought the guy was hot and she guessed she could see why. He was tall and had dark brown eyes and very white teeth. He always looked tan and he had one of those smiles that only went up on one side and left you unsure of his intentions. He was good looking, almost too good looking. His friend, Hulk Norton, was standing behind him watching and listening with a goofy smile on his face. He was a really weird guy, nicknamed after the Incredible Hulk, not just because he had liked the comic book character as a kid, but because he was huge and, except for not turning green, there was a resemblance. He never said much. The strong and silent type, but definitely not handsome.

"I hear you found a letter on the corpse," Tommy said with his little sneer.

"Yeah, I did," Sarah answered, "So?"

"But the police say they never saw a letter."

"I saw it. I reported it. I can't help it that someone took it." She was in full defensive mode.

"That's a little odd, that only you saw it," he said. She decided that she really didn't like that sideways smile.

"Are you calling me a liar?"

"That wouldn't be polite, and besides, as I said, you're pretty. Never tell a pretty girl she's lying."

He turned and sauntered away. Sarah noticed it was in the twins' direction. They squealed their hellos to him. Sarah would have thought he'd be embarrassed, but he seemed just fine with it.

Jake, Rob, and Sarah got blue ribbons for their racing efforts. Amazing that a little bit of cheesy satin could make them feel so good.

"See, I told you," Jake said. "One down and the rest to go. We'll have a room full of these by the end of the summer." He waved his ribbon triumphantly.

Sarah was feeling good. People were congratulating her right and left. Rachel Young made a real point of telling her how wonderful the race was.

"I'm glad you beat old Tommy," she said. "He needs a bit of beating."

They stayed until most of the people had left. Then Jake and Rob accepted a ride home with the twins, which Sarah declined. She started to walk home by herself when Tommy Emmerson pulled up beside her in his car.

"Want a ride?" he asked.

She was still annoyed by that remark about her needing to fix herself up, but he had called her pretty, and had told her it was a good race. She hesitated a minute because she really didn't want to ride with him. But she didn't exactly know how to say no.

"Okay," she said, hesitantly. "Thanks."

Sarah felt awkward sitting next to Tommy in the front seat. What do you say to a seventeen-year-old that doesn't sound dumb? She was just glad that, for some reason, Hulk wasn't around.

She shouldn't have worried. Tommy didn't wait for her to start a conversation. He told her that there was always an element of luck in a race and that they had been lucky, but to watch out next time, he'd be gunning for them. He mentioned several times that he had won more first-place ribbons than anyone on the lake.

"I think I've won more than anyone ever did," he said. "Someday, I'm going to check the archives on that."

"What archives?" she asked.

"Don't suppose you would know. I keep forgetting you're just a little tadpole." His voice took on an instructive tone. "The club has records, and the paper too, they have this whole room they call a morgue and it has records of everything that ever happened around here."

Now that little tidbit was interesting. She knew about morgues in big city newspapers, but she hadn't imagined their little weekly would have one. It could contain some very interesting information about way more than how many races Tommy Emmerson had won.

When he left her off at the back of her cottage, Jennifer was just coming out the door. She waved as she spotted the car. When Sarah got out, she stopped waving. Tommy hadn't even noticed her, he sped out of the yard at his usual Nascar speed.

"What were you doing riding in Tommy's car?" Jennifer demanded.

"We won," Sarah said. "We came in first."

"Super. I repeat, what were you doing in Tommy's car?"

"Tommy offered me a ride. So what?"

"Why on God's earth would he do that?" she asked with disdain.

"Well, he told me I was pretty, maybe that's why."

Jennifer looked at her sister, at a loss for words. Sarah didn't bother to tell her the part about needing some fixing up.

It was obvious that Jennifer was going someplace. Her makeup was perfect and she had her uselessly tiny purse on her shoulder. But she turned and followed Sarah when she walked into the cottage.

"What were you doing even talking to Tommy Emmerson?" she asked.

"He was talking to me, can I help that?"

"What is he, some kind of pedophile? First Megan and now you?"

"You're not that much older than me," Sarah said. "And, besides, it's your friend you're calling names, not mine."

"Everyone's calling you a big liar, you know," Jennifer said, her eyes narrowing, "Going around talking about some letter you saw just to get attention. It's pathetic. It is such an embarrassment to have you for a sister."

An embarrassment? Most of what her sister said to her, Sarah just ignored. But, an embarrassment?

That did it. As far as she was concerned, Jennifer really had nothing to say that she wanted to hear. She walked into the bedroom. But then, she stopped in front of the mirror and looked at herself. Pretty? Needed fixing up? She guessed the latter was true. She wore her hair in a pony tail and didn't wear any makeup. She had a dirty sweatshirt over her swimsuit and, on her feet, some really old sneakers. She had never paid much attention to how she looked. She had called Jake a swan for looking awkward on land; she supposed she looked pretty awkward too.

Well, there was nothing she could do about it right now. She went out front and looked at the boats. The canoe had been patched, it was sitting in the water and there didn't appear to be any leaks. The motor was back on the boat. Now if she returned to the Big Island, she could make a quick getaway. Not that she had any intention of going there again.

Her dad was gone. He had wanted to come to the race, but it was a long trip home and he had to be in court the next morning. Normally, on his weekend trips, he would take Friday or Monday off, but this had been a last-minute thing. Sarah understood. But she wished she could have watched her parents say goodbye. It might have shown her what was going on. They had been just a little too polite to each other. Not that they weren't always polite, but this was different.

The day after the race, Sarah's mother sent her to the store across the lake for some tarragon for her chicken salad. Frankly, Sarah didn't think it made all that much difference, but she wanted to try out the canoe anyway.

She tied up at the store dock and walked up the hill to the general store where they had a little bit of everything. They even had penny candy in jars, which Sarah used to love as a kid. Of course, it wasn't a penny anymore; actually, it never was, not in Sarah's lifetime, but she would still, occasionally, reach in and choose some of her favorites.

There was always someone she knew at the store. Sarah said hi to the little kids around the candy jars. And Mrs. Peterson was at the cash register. Sarah had known her all her life. She was a big woman who had a laugh that boomed all over the store. Mr. Peterson, on the other hand, was a thin little man who never smiled.

The person she didn't expect to see was Chief McCarry. Sarah couldn't remember ever seeing him in the store. But maybe she just wouldn't have noticed him before their recent encounter.

"Hello, Sarah," he said. She had intended to avoid him and was, in fact, trying to move behind some shelves.

"Hello." She almost said Mr. McCarry. Was she supposed to call him 'Chief?'

"You doing okay?" he asked. He was trying for a friendly voice, which didn't quite work.

"Sure," she answered.

She walked over to the fresh herbs and got the tarragon, then figured she deserved a soda for her efforts and picked one up. The chief was checking out. He hadn't bought much, some cigarettes and a bottle of root beer. Sarah didn't know anyone who drank root beer.

There was another man looking at the cold drinks with her. He was tall and dark, but pretty normal looking. She thought about what Rob had said, that there were strangers around that they never noticed. This guy was a stranger and she normally wouldn't have noticed him. It didn't seem like he could be the island man, though. He certainly wasn't her image of that man—he wasn't hairy and horrible. He looked like someone who took regular showers. He definitely wasn't the island man. He was just in there for a six-pack of beer.

When it was her turn at the register, Mrs. Peterson, who always had a little chat with everyone, congratulated her on the sailing race. It was a topic Sarah enjoyed. She didn't expect that Chief McCarry would still be on the porch when she went out. But he was.

"You thought of anything else you can tell us?" he asked her.

"No. I told you everything," she said.

"Not at first, you didn't. Maybe your memory still has some gaps."

"Look, I'm having a tough enough time. Everyone thinks I lied about seeing the letter." She realized she shouldn't be talking to the police chief like this.

"I'm not surprised to hear that." He sat down on the steps and motioned her to sit down beside him. "Let's talk about that for a minute." He took a swig of his root beer. "You didn't lie. I know that. Traces of paper were found. But the thing is, you were the only one to see it. There wasn't any evidence of anyone else being near the body. So, if you took that letter, you need to let me know. Now. You won't be in any trouble. I'll see to that. But we need that letter."

"I put it back. I realized I had done something wrong by even touching it. I put it back just the way I found it."

"It's really important," he said. "We don't have much here. It all happened so long ago." He was looking straight at her, his eyes on hers. It was making her very uncomfortable.

"I understand that. I'd give it to you if I had it, but I don't." She sounded a little desperate, even to herself.

His small attempt at friendliness disappeared. He nodded as if confirming something to himself. He didn't believe her, that was obvious. How do you prove you didn't do something? She wished she had taken the letter and could just hand it over. But she hadn't.

"I need you to keep what I told you confidential, that we found physical evidence of the letter," he told her as he got up. "We like to keep some things to ourselves."

"But that would let people know I was telling the truth," she protested, thinking about what her sister had said.

"So would handing over the letter." He gave her one last look and walked away.

What could she say to that? Maybe she needed to go back to the island and look for it herself. She shuddered at the thought.

On one side of the store was a little addition. It was a bait shop where people could pick up worms for fishing. A few years ago, they had sold them in the store, but when they started carrying things like produce and herbs, they moved the worms outside. Sarah noticed two men she had never seen before picking out their bait. Rob was right. There were strangers all over the place. Sarah was pretty sure neither of these men were the island man: they were talking to each other. The island man had to be a loner, a big-time loner, living on an island all by himself. But funny she hadn't noticed strangers before. She would notice them from now on.

11

At least Rob and Jake believed Sarah about the letter. It would not have occurred to them to doubt her word. They knew Sarah Ramsey. She was not into lying and Rob liked telling her what a terrible poker player she would be, she had that kind of open face that made sure she never got away with anything.

After talking about it for awhile, Jake began to think he had seen the letter case too. He hadn't. When they first saw the bones, they were too shocked to notice anything like that. But Sarah was grateful to anyone who didn't doubt her.

Jake wasn't spending as much time with the twins now. Rob still went over there, and they called him up a lot. His mother was getting tired of taking messages from them. Cell phones didn't work very well around the lake, one more complaint the twins had about being there.

On the afternoon of July Fourth, Sarah, Rob, and Jake had taken out her canoe and turned it upside down. They couldn't have explained why they had always thought that was so much fun. They had been doing it forever. When they were younger they liked to swim under it, where there was air and their voices sounded weird when they talked. For some reason, telling secrets there seemed much more important. Now, they climbed on top to sit and talk, occasionally diving off and swimming around when they got hot.

It was a sticky day and they sat and dangled their feet in the water, talking about everything and nothing and feeling very lazy, when suddenly Rob imparted some news that made Sarah actually glad he was still visiting the twins.

"Their great-grandmother's coming today," he announced.

"Rearden, you'e such a dork. You're their personal planner now?" Jake asked, his resentment obvious.

"Today?" Sarah turned to Rob, all feeling of lethargy gone. "I guess it would be polite to go over and meet her?" She made it a question, but there was no question in her mind. That was one person she really wanted to talk to.

"Since when are you Miss Meet-and-Greet?" asked Jake.

"I hear she's a little spacey," said Rob, "so don't get your hopes up. It's not Alzheimer's, but she's forgetful."

"She's not so far gone that she couldn't make the decision to come up here when she heard about us finding the bones. If anyone knows anything, she does," Sarah pointed out.

"So what are you going to do?" asked Jake. "Interrogate an old lady?"

"Asking a couple of questions is not an interrogation," Sarah insisted. "What time is she coming?"

"Ramsey, you are so psyched about this." said Rob. "The twins aren't going to be fooled by this sudden friendship."

"You're actually attributing some brain cells to them," she said. "Just tell me the time."

He laughed and told her they would arrive in time for dinner. She noticed he didn't bother to defend the twins on their lack of intelligence.

And anyway, she had a plan. It was the kill-two-birds-with-one-stone kind of thing. She was going to have to swallow some pride to make it work. But her pride had been taking a lot of hits lately. She was getting used to it.

At three o'clock, she sauntered over to the Frasers' cottage. This time she walked the long way around and spotted a strange car in their driveway.

She went around to the front porch; there are certain protocols to be practiced at Loon Lake.

And there they were, all sitting there, Mrs. Fraser, the twins, a tiny little white-haired woman and a man she presumed to be Dr. Fraser.

"Oh," she said, as though surprised. "I'm so sorry to be interrupting. I didn't know you had company." Sometimes Sarah actually did lie, just a little. And this was her new first rule of investigation, that sometimes you need to slide around the truth in order to find out the whole truth.

"Sarah, dear," said Mrs. Fraser, standing up and greeting her with a smile. "How nice to see you. Come, join us. Let me introduce you. This is the girls' great-grandmother, Mrs. Gerard. And their father, Dr. Fraser."

Sarah did the proper hand-shaking thing—she was getting used to it. But she wondered why mothers never related anything to themselves. This was Mrs. Fraser's husband and her grandmother. Sarah's mom did the same thing, everything was about the kids.

Dr. Fraser sat a little apart from the others. He had his nose buried in a magazine or maybe a medical journal. He barely acknowledged Sarah with a nod and went back to his reading.

They all chatted a minute, the requisite small talk. Mrs. Gerard wasn't saying anything until Mrs. Fraser mentioned that she looked tired.

"It's a long train ride up here," said Mrs. Gerard.

The twins and Dr. Fraser immediately corrected her.

"You came in a car, Nana," said Dr. Fraser.

Melissa laughed. "Nana, there's no train around here."

"A car, Nana. A car," said Megan.

"Of course," said Mrs. Gerard. She looked a little embarrassed. "We used to come by train sometimes. I always liked that."

"Girls, maybe you'd like to take Sarah inside. I'm sure she's not interested in sitting around and talking to all us old folks," Mrs. Fraser suggested.

The twins looked at each other. Sarah figured they were weighing which was worse, being with her or more sitting around with their parents. She guessed she won. They stood up and Sarah followed them inside. They took her to their bedroom. This was both good and bad. It would help her in one way, but she wanted to talk to Mrs. Gerard. However, she was in the house, so maybe her turn with the grandmother could come later. She really preferred to talk to her alone, anyway.

This was definitely a cottage bedroom, but bigger and nicer than Sarah's. It had white rattan twin beds and a dresser to match. It was as messy as Sarah's—there were clothes on every surface and on the floor. The twins might always look model neat, but they left a wake. That actually made her feel slightly better about them.

She purposefully walked over to the mirror and looked at herself.

"I'm a mess, aren't I?"

That got their attention. They looked at each other, obviously agreeing with Sarah, but hesitant about actually saying it.

"Someone told me recently that I needed some fixing up." Now Sarah turned to face them.

"That was rather rude," said Melissa.

"Rude, but true." Sarah turned back to the mirror. "So how about it? You two are so put together. Beautiful, really." She almost choked on that last part. It was true, but she didn't like telling them that. She felt like such a phony. She watched them in the mirror as they smiled.

"Can you do an extreme makeover on me? What, for instance, can I do with this hair?" She pulled off her scrunchie and her hair made its wild escape into every direction.

"Omigod," said Megan. "I had no idea your hair was so thick."

"And curly," said Melissa.

"Some would say frizzy," Sarah said. They didn't argue.

Sarah didn't think they really wanted to help her, but she didn't think they could resist the challenge. They sat her down and Melissa picked up a brush and Megan a comb. They were not necessarily gentle, but somehow, between them, they sprayed and combed and brushed and gelled and managed to make her hair look really good. Then they started on the makeup.

"The idea is to look like you don't have any on," Megan informed her.

"It's the eyes. You can really do a lot to the eyes and if you only wear a light lip gloss, nobody thinks you have any makeup on at all," said Melissa.

They now turned her away from the mirror, so she couldn't see what was happening. She had a few moments of fear. What would they do to her face?

"So, your great-grandmother really did come up here. And it's all about the skeleton on the island?" Sarah asked, in what she hoped was a conversational tone.

"Yeah, she hasn't mentioned it yet, but that's what it's all about," said Melissa.

"After years of not allowing anyone to talk about the hotel fire or the island, now she's here," said Megan.

"The trip's made her really tired," said Melissa.

"Do you suppose she's going out to the Big Island?" asked Sarah.

Whatever they were doing to her eyebrows stopped for a minute. Since it had involved both pain and plucking, Sarah wasn't sorry. They looked at each other. Sarah had noticed they did that a lot. She wondered what it would be like, looking for confirmation of your own thoughts from someone who looked exactly like yourself. Weird.

"I never thought of that," said Megan.

"Maybe we'll all go," said Melissa.

"But what if the bones are still there?" asked Megan.

"Oh, the bones are long gone," Sarah told her. "The police have already done tests on them and everything."

"Then I'd go," said Megan. "I'd like to see the hotel."

"There's not much left," Sarah said, "just rubble."

"Wait a minute." Melissa put down the tweezers she was using to torture Sarah's eyebrows and ran from the room. She was back in a minute. She shoved a photo album onto

Sarah's lap and turned the pages until she found what she wanted.

"This is my mom's lake album. She brought it up because she wanted to see all these places again. Here's what I was looking for."

The whole page was filled with pictures of the hotel, a few old faded black-and-white photos and a couple of brochure pictures.

The building was beautiful, small but stately. It was made of white frame with a huge porch curved all around the front and sides. There was a red shingle roof. It had been three stories high and the grounds around it were filled with wide lawns and shrubs and flowers.

There was a close-up picture of four people sitting in wicker chairs on the porch in old-fashioned clothes. Other people were in the background, holding cocktail glasses and standing or sitting on a porch swing or in rocking chairs. The scene looked like something out of *The Great Gatsby*.

"That's Nana and my great uncle, when they were little, and those are their parents, our great-greats. Raymond Steward was his name. He's the one who owned the hotel. He was killed in the fire," Melissa said pointing out each person sitting in the chairs.

"The hotel was beautiful," Sarah told her.

"It was pretty, wasn't it? They had all kinds of boats for the guests and they even had horses to ride. There were trails to follow all over the island," said Megan.

Sarah wondered if maybe she had been on one of the horse trails and didn't know it.

"It looks like such a romantic place, doesn't it?" said Melissa. The three of them stared at the pictures.

"People dressed up for dinner," said Megan. "And some people spent the whole summer there." She had a dreamy look on her face.

"And they had musicians come and play on Friday and Saturday nights," said Melissa.

"I really really wish I could have seen it," said Megan.

"We've heard some wonderful stories about things that happened there. Like couples who got engaged or even married," said Melissa.

They continued working on Sarah during the last bit of conversation. Suddenly they turned her around and she could see herself in the mirror.

"Wow," she said. It wasn't her. It was some new version of her, but it wasn't her. She didn't look made up, but the eyes that were staring back at her looked so big, so dark.

Her hair fell in soft waves around her face and she had color in her cheeks that she had never seen there before.

"Come on," said Melissa. "Let's show you off."

"We did a fabulous job. Maybe we should start some sort of business or something," said Megan.

They dragged her out of the chair, eager to impress their family with their talent. Sarah felt a little silly, like some sort of new toy about to be displayed.

When they stepped down onto the porch, Mrs. Fraser stood up.

"My goodness, Sarah, I hardly recognized you. What have you done to yourself?"

"She didn't do a thing," said Megan. "We did it."

"Pretty impressive, huh?" said Melissa.

"She's beautiful," said Mrs. Fraser. "I can't wait to see what Jake and Rob will say when they see you, Sarah. Their eyes will pop out."

"Whoops, maybe we made a mistake here," said Megan peevishly.

Melissa was frowning at Sarah. "Yeah, maybe we did."

"I think I'd better make an appointment with you two," said Mrs. Fraser, laughing. "I was always such a tomboy growing up. You girls know so much more about all this beauty business than I do."

"I think you're fine just the way you are," said Dr. Fraser. Sarah turned and looked at him, at the way he was smiling at his wife, at the way he looked at her when he said it, at her quick smile back at him. Sarah hadn't been hearing anything like that from her parents in awhile. She felt a quick prick of tears behind her eyes. Her parents used to act like that.

"Come over here, dear," said Mrs. Gerard from her chair. Sarah walked over to her. Mrs. Gerard gestured to Sarah to lean down, then she reached up and touched her hair. "Yes," she said. "Very pretty. Patsy was always pretty."

Sarah looked toward Mrs. Fraser for some explanation. She only shook her head sadly.

Oh God, this wasn't going to be easy. Sarah needed information from this woman and how was she going to get any if she didn't make any sense? Sarah couldn't think of any reply to her comment, so she started talking about getting home for dinner.

She thanked the twins, but they were still frowning at her. "I'm sorry I interrupted your visit," she said to Mrs. Gerard. But she wasn't really listening.

Walking back along the shore, Sarah wondered if she could ever get any real information from the old woman. But she had come up here after she heard about the body—she had to have been making some sense then.

What Sarah wasn't prepared for was the reaction she got when she walked in her door. Her mother was setting the table. She stopped and stared. "You look lovely," she said. Jennifer was flipping channels. The remote froze in her hand and she got up from the couch.

"What happened to you?" she demanded in an angry voice.

"The twins are good for something after all," Sarah said.

"What happened to your frizz?" Jennifer demanded, as she walked toward Sarah and reached out and touched her hair.

"I'm not exactly sure," Sarah admitted. "I wasn't allowed to watch the whole thing."

"Absolutely lovely," said her mother, looking pensive. "I wish your father could see you."

Conrad greeted her as he normally did. He didn't care what she looked like and she must have smelled the same. Just then she heard a call from outside. Jake, Rob, and Sarah still did that, got close to one of their cottages and called out.

"Hey, Ramsey," yelled Jake. "You home?"

She went out to the porch. Both Rob and Jake were in Jake's row boat. "Come on in," she yelled back.

That in itself was unusual. They didn't spend much time in each other's cottages. The outdoors was their world.

The boys tied up the boat and came across the lawn to the porch. Sarah waited for them. Jennifer had followed her and was standing with her arms folded watching her. She was fuming.

"Good," thought Sarah.

"Whoa," said Jake who came in the door first. "What happened to you?"

Sarah didn't answer. She was looking at Rob. But he didn't say a word. He just smiled. She loved it. It was a moment she'd never forget. And it did something to her. She felt good about herself, for all the wrong reasons, maybe, but still the feeling was there. Seeing Jennifer's face was so gratifying, and seeing the boys' reactions was icing on the cake. She felt pretty and it was a wonderful feeling. However, she knew something that the others didn't know. There was no way she could duplicate this new her. She hadn't even seen how the twins did their magic. In order to maintain this look, she'd have to hire the twins to make her up every day. And look how long it had taken. No way was she was going to spend that kind of time on herself. Tomorrow she'd have the ponytail again and life would go on as before. But tonight, she felt like a princess. And she couldn't have asked for it on a better night.

Everyone on the lake went to the Beach Club for the Fourth of July fireworks. They wouldn't start until dusk, and dusk came late this time of year. But everyone would begin heading over after dinner.

"I see you're about to eat," said Rob. "Jake and I are going to grab a hot dog at the club and get a good place. But I guess you can't come." He looked at Sarah's mother.

"Of course she can't come," said Jennifer. "We're just about to sit down."

"We're not having much, just a salad," said Jean Ramsey. She was looking at Sarah in a strange way. "You can go with the boys and get a hot dog if you want to."

"Then why do I have to eat dinner here?" demanded Jennifer.

"You don't. Go ahead if you want to," her mother told her.

Obviously Jennifer didn't have anywhere to go. Her friends must be planning to meet after dinner. She looked thoroughly disgruntled.

"Well, it wouldn't be nice to leave you all alone, Mother," she said.

That one didn't even begin to fool her mother.

It was a wonderful night, clear, a perfect temperature, a hint of a breeze. There'd be a million stars when the sun went down. They rowed over and got a good docking place because it was so early. Jake had brought blankets and they spread them on the ground right by the shore, right near where the barge would set off the fireworks.

Then, having claimed their territory, they wandered over to get their hot dogs. People started coming soon and Sarah was luxuriating in everyone's reaction to her.

When the Fraser family appeared it was even better. She kept giving the twins credit for her transformation, but they weren't pleased.

The Frasers had brought beach chairs and they set them a little apart from the mass of people so that Mrs. Gerard wouldn't get jostled. The girls didn't stay with their parents long. And, surprisingly, the boys didn't go running after them. Megan and Melissa had their group of admirers, anyway, mostly Jennifer's friends. Tommy Emmerson was front and center. Sarah was looking forward to him noticing her. After all, he had seen her potential when nobody else had. Not that she wanted anything to do with him. He was still annoying as far as she was concerned—conceited, rude, and way too old for her. But Rachel noticed her.

"Look at you, Sarah, you're gorgeous," she called out.

And when Tommy turned to look, it was everything Sarah could have hoped for, especially when she heard him tell Jennifer that she'd better watch out for that little sister of hers. Even Hulk Norton did a double-take.

The club had hired a three-piece band, some college kids, who made for their lack of skill with their enthusiasm. They played old familiar patriotic music that set up the mood. The little kids were all dancing and jumping in front of the bandstand.

Loon Lake had the best fireworks around, so everyone from the area came, lake people, year-round people, and people from nearby lakes. Everyone was welcomed. But it was getting congested.

Sarah was looking at the crowd when she happened to spot her mother crossing the lawn. Beverly Fraser stood up, obviously inviting her to join them. Sarah was surprised when her mom shook her head and barely stopped to talk. She chose, instead, to sit with the Spencers, who Sarah knew she wasn't all that fond of. What happened to the new-best-friend thing?

At one point the Frasers got up and went to talk to some people, leaving Mrs. Gerard by herself. Sarah scrambled over there as fast as she could–this might be her only chance to see her alone.

She re-introduced herself, but Mrs. Gerard seemed to remember her, so she sat down on the ground by her chair.

"It's a great night for the fireworks, isn't it?" Sarah started, for something to say.

Mrs. Gerard had a really sweet smile. "Yes," she agreed. "But it usually is. We had a so many wonderful Fourths on the lake in my day."

"Did you ever see any loons?" Sarah asked, more of the making conversation, but she actually wanted to know.

"Of course," Mrs. Gerard said. "They're interesting birds. Come to think of it, I haven't seen any today."

"They're gone. They aren't here anymore." Sarah told her.

"Where did they go?" She sat up and looked around as though she would spot one.

"Probably the whole environmental thing," Sarah said.

"Oh." Mrs. Gerard looked sadly out at the water. "It's still a lovely lake though, isn't it?" she said.

"I love every drop of it." Sarah told her.

She smiled again. "I'm so glad you feel that way. I'm so glad people still feel that way. After my father died, we even spent some winters up here. Things were difficult for my mother financially for awhile. It was cold and uncomfortable, our cottage wasn't well insulated. But I loved it here, even in the winter. It was more important to my mother to keep the cottage than the house in town. I was always glad about that." She began to ease herself out of her chair. Sarah stood up and helped her.

"I would like to visit the ladies' room," she said, looking around.

Dr. Fraser came back just then. He had overheard what she said.

"I'll be glad to take her," Sarah said quickly. Mrs. Gerard grabbed onto Sarah's arm and let her lead her up to the clubhouse.

"Wait for me?" she said when they got to the restroom door.

"Of course."

Sarah waited for her just around the building so she wouldn't get in the way of the door. But Mrs. Gerard was gone quite awhile and the fireworks were getting ready to start. Sarah wanted to go back to her friends. So she went back around the corner and was about to open the restroom door when she heard voices, just around the other corner.

There was a deep voice of a man trying to talk softly, but it was gruff and it carried. She heard a small, gentle, woman's voice so soft she couldn't make out any words, and then his voice again, saying the word. It was the one word Sarah had been most sure about in the letter, a word she had hardly ever heard, and now was hearing again. Weird. It was asked like a question in that deep male voice.

"Caveat?"

Then she heard a small moan.

She rushed around the corner. Mrs. Gerard was on the ground. People were suddenly coming toward her from all directions, but Sarah got there first.

"Are you all right?" she asked, trying to lift her up.

With Sarah's help, Mrs. Gerard managed to sit, leaning against the wall. "Just let me rest a minute," she said.

"What happened?" Sarah asked her.

Mrs. Gerard didn't answer and it was only then that Sarah looked around for the voice she had heard. But people were crowding in on them. Mrs. Gerard tried to wave them away.

After a few minutes, she attempted to stand up. Sarah knew she was uncomfortable with the people around her, even with their sympathetic concern.

"Take me back to the chairs," she said.

"Are you sure you're ready?" Sarah asked. But Mrs. Gerard insisted. Sarah took her arm and they walked slowly back through the crowd.

"What happened?" Sarah asked again.

"I'm not sure," Mrs. Gerard said. "Sometimes my mind gets confused. But somebody was talking to me. I thought it was—I must have felt a little faint."

They were approaching the chairs where Dr. and Mrs. Fraser were sitting. Mrs. Gerard grabbed Sarah's arm. "Don't say anything, not just yet. Not about someone talking to me. Please?" She looked at Sarah with pleading eyes.

"I won't, not if you don't want me to." It seemed a strange thing to keep secret.

"Don't say anything about me feeling faint either. They worry about me so. I didn't hurt myself. I'm fine."

Just then the first blast of rockets went up. There were the usual *oohs* and *ahs* from the crowd. Mrs. Fraser stood up and took Mrs. Gerard's arm and settled her into her chair.

"Thank you so much, Sarah," said Mrs. Fraser. "You were very kind to help Nana."

Mrs. Gerard gave Sarah one last look and put her finger to her lips in the universal "be quiet" sign.

Sarah said goodbye and hurried through the crowd to Jake's blanket.

There was a lot of noise, with the music, the fireworks, and the people shouting when a good one went up.

Sarah had promised Mrs. Gerard she wouldn't tell anyone. But when the first lull came, when they were setting up more rockets, Sarah did let Rob and Jake in on the fact that she had heard Mrs. Gerard talking to a man. She didn't feel she was betraying her promise. She wouldn't say anything about her fainting or about her thinking she knew the man. Sarah figured Mrs. Gerard was afraid she had just imagined him. But she hadn't. Sarah had heard the voice. It wasn't fair to keep the boys entirely out of it. They were in on this too. And Sarah wanted to know what they thought. Their heads were close together and Sarah was whispering as she told them.

"You can't tell anyone," Sarah insisted. "She really made me promise not to tell, but I need your help in trying to figure this out."

They swore they wouldn't say a word to anyone. And she believed them.

"Caveat is an odd word," Sarah said. Now she wasn't whispering anymore. "And he used it as a question. And his tone of voice was strange. He was talking about the letter, I know he was. I wish I had never seen that letter. I wish we had never found that body."

It was especially crowded so close to the water, people almost on top of them. It wasn't surprising that someone heard what she said.

"She's still talking about that letter," came a voice from the crowd.

"Non-existent letter, you mean," said somebody else.

Sarah was sorry she had brought it up and was glad when the fireworks started their grand finale and people paid attention to that.

Of course, everyone left at the same time and there was a lot of jostling and bumping, and "excuse me's" on the dock as people went to their boats.

It had been an interesting night. Sarah could talk to Mrs. Gerard after all. And she would. Mrs. Gerard thought she had recognized someone, the same someone who had said the word. It had been a deep voice, not unlike the island man when he shouted at her. But she couldn't be sure. There is a big difference between a shout and a whisper. But even a whisper can sound menacing.

It had been a very satisfying night for Sarah with her new look. But Cinderella's coach eventually turned back into a pumpkin and Sarah went back to being herself the very next day. It was, however, a Sarah with a new direction. Mrs. Gerard knew a lot of the things they needed to find out if they were ever to discover anything about the island and the fire and the man buried in the shallow grave. Sarah knew she could talk to her and she would. She had the answers to many of their questions.

12

Early the next morning, Sarah's mother announced that she was going to do the laundry. Sarah and Jennifer were to bring her their dirty clothes before they could go out. Sarah had worn white shorts to the fireworks. White shorts can only be worn once. They were on the top of the pile when she emptied the hamper.

Jennifer always acted like she would get a disease if she touched anything Sarah had worn, so she had daintily removed her own clothes from their mutual pile and carried them to the washing machine.

"Be sure you check the pockets," Sarah's mother called out, as she always did.

Sarah almost didn't bother to check those white shorts, she hadn't carried anything with her last night. But, dutifully, she did, and she pulled out a small piece of paper with torn edges that looked like it had been ripped out of a spiral notebook.

It was folded over once. She opened it and read.

Forget about the letter. No one will ever believe you and you'll be sorry if you don't stop talking about it. Forget about the body. Forget all of it.

When she read the letter to herself, she heard, in her mind, the voice she had heard last night. But there was no guarantee that the man had written the note. It could have been anyone.

She put the note way down in the pocket of the shorts she had on that morning and carried her dirty clothes to her mother.

As soon as she could, she escaped any additional chores and called Rob and Jake to meet her at their tree.

She showed them the note.

"Jeez. Who wrote this?" asked Jake.

"Obviously, I don't know," she told him.

"This is a threat, I mean a real threat. You can't fool around now, you've got to go to the police with this," said Rob. He looked really worried.

"I know what it is." Their stating the obvious was making her annoyed. "But I hate talking to the police. They don't believe anything I say."

"Doesn't matter. You have to go," said Rob.

"If someone put it in your pocket last night, then it was somebody who got up close to you," said Jake. "Do you remember anyone pushing you or anything?"

"Everyone was pushing everyone," Sarah said.

They talked more, but Sarah wasn't finding the boys very helpful and they were making her more nervous than she had been before. She didn't need that.

They offered to go to the police with her, but she didn't accept their offer. This was something she'd do herself.

She went home and told her mom that she was going to the Peterson's store across the lake and she even asked her mother if she needed anything. Big mistake, because, of course, mothers always need something, and Sarah hadn't had any intention of going to the store.

She headed her canoe in that direction, but as she approached the opposite shore she turned and went toward her true destination, the police station.

Chief McCarry wasn't there and she didn't want to talk to Officer Ellis—no point in having to repeat everything twice.

So she went to the store, got her mother's stuff, and indulged herself with a candy bar. She wondered how long it had been since the skinny twins had actually sunk their teeth into chocolate or caramel. That made her enjoy it all the more.

When she walked out of the store the chief was sitting in his car leaning against his open window.

"I heard you came to see me," he said.

"How did you know I'd be here?" she asked.

He smiled and that made Sarah nervous. She almost changed her mind about telling him anything, but then he said, "Officer Ellis told me you were heading this way and I saw your canoe. See what great detective work I do?"

She showed him the note. "Someone slipped it in my pocket at the fireworks last night."

He read it several times. "You know you could have written this yourself, just to get me off your back."

"Except I didn't," Sarah said indignantly.

He didn't believe her, he made that obvious. Still, he insisted on keeping the note. She knew what it said, so she guessed that was all right.

Since her dad was still calling every night, she told her mother she wanted to talk to him the next time he called, and that evening she told him about the note and about hearing someone talk about the letter, or at least using the word "caveat." She really wanted to tell him that Mrs. Gerard had maybe recognized someone, but a promise was a promise.

"The police chief thinks I have the letter," she blurted out.

"You don't really know that," her father said.

"He wasn't being subtle." She tried to repeat his words, or at least let her father know how the conversation went. But maybe you had to be there.

"Well, I've been trying to make arrangements to take some time off and come up there. But I'm still in court and it depends on how that goes. In the meantime, I'll give the chief a call."

"No, don't do that. Let's just wait and see what happens," Sarah said. She really didn't want the chief any more angry with her than he seemed to be already.

"You need to be careful, Sarah. Very careful. This note thing has me worried. I don't know what's going on, but I can't stand the idea that someone's giving you a warning like that. Watch yourself. This could be very dangerous. I keep thinking of that man chasing you off the island. You've got to avoid situations where anything like that could happen."

"Maybe it's just some kind of joke," she suggested, hopefully. "Some kid's idea of humor."

"Maybe. But let's not take any chances."

After that he wanted to talk to her mother again. Sarah had purposefully removed herself from the room every time he called. She wanted them to solve whatever problems they had. She walked outside and waited until they were through.

Sarah believed in coincidence. Sometimes things just happen along side each other. But, after awhile, she couldn't convince herself that seeing Chief McCarry's car everywhere she went was a coincidence. When she went to the store, he was there. When she came out of the Beach Club, he was there. When she went to the mailbox, he was there. She would have had to spend all her time in the middle of the lake to avoid him. It was a good thing that she actually did spend much of her time in the middle of the lake. But it was worrying her. How in the world could she ever convince him she didn't have the letter?

That wasn't the only thing happening around the lake. All of a sudden families were telling people about missing relatives. The Hendersons, who had a cottage across the lake, told everyone about a remote uncle who had disappeared some seventy years ago. He had been a wanderer who didn't get along with his family and had been gone for three years here and four years there before he disappeared for good. He had told everyone he was going to Australia, so nobody ever reported him missing. They supposed he had just found a new life. Now they began to wonder.

And the Acuffs, whose cottage was near the Beach Club, also had a missing person. Except it was a woman who eloped with a scoundrel and was never seen again. The police assured them that the bones belonged to a man.

But there was a lot of delving back into family histories. Some interesting stories were circulating. It seemed that almost every family had some secrets, and now they were coming out.

It made Sarah curious about her own family history. And she found out some things about her mother's family she never knew before. That didn't count because her mother hadn't grown up at the lake. But she had a great-great-someone who had been hanged as a horse thief out West. Who would have thought?

All these discussions about family histories turned out to be a good thing. It became easy to bring conversations around to the past. The next time Sarah visited the Frasers, she didn't even have to introduce the subject.

She went with Rob and Jake. Mrs. Gerard and Mrs. Fraser were sitting on the porch, so it was fine with Sarah when the boys went down to the dock to dote on the twins. They still hadn't kicked the habit entirely.

Sarah sat down next to Mrs. Gerard, who reached over and patted her arm. "Such a sweet child," she said.

It was difficult for Sarah to immediately tell if Mrs. Gerard's mind was in the here and now. She was staring at the water, but she did that a lot.

"The loons are all gone," she said. Tears started to fall down her face.

"It's all right, Nana," said Mrs. Fraser. She turned to Sarah. "She's not having a good day today, I'm afraid. She's feeling very sad. The crying's been going on all morning. And now she's drifting off again."

Sarah didn't think Mrs. Gerard actually was drifting. She knew what she was talking about. But she didn't understand the crying. And she didn't like the way Mrs. Fraser was talking about her as if she wasn't there.

"You miss them too," Mrs. Gerard said to Sarah.

"Actually, Mrs. Gerard, I've never seen one. At least you had the chance to experience them."

"That's true, isn't it? How sad to have never seen them."

Mrs. Fraser was looking from one of them to the other.

"What are you talking about?" she asked Sarah.

"Loons," both Mrs. Gerard and Sarah spoke at the same time. Then Sarah laughed and Mrs. Gerard did too. It was like an emotional faucet, crying off, laughing on.

Mrs. Fraser smiled rather tentatively.

"Sarah, would you mind staying here and keeping Nana company? I really do have a couple of things I need to do."

"Not at all," Sarah said. She had hoped for a minute alone with Mrs. Gerard. Once again Mrs. Gerard patted Sarah's arm.

"Are you okay?" Sarah asked her.

"I'm not as bad as they think," she answered, after Mrs. Fraser had left the room.

"Can we talk about the man you saw the night of the fireworks?" Sarah asked.

"I'm very confused about that," Mrs. Gerard said. "I'm not sure at all. It looked like Paul. But then again, it didn't."

"Paul who?"

Mrs. Gerard looked at Sarah as though she should know.

"You remember," she said.

"No, Mrs. Gerard. I don't."

"Patsy knew. I'm sure Patsy knew." Who was Patsy? Sarah wondered. Should she ask her? Was she someone from the Big Island?

Mrs. Gerard was drifting. Maybe if Sarah just waited, she'd come back.

"Patsy is a pretty name," Sarah said for lack of anything else to say.

"You're not Patsy, are you?" Mrs. Gerard looked right at Sarah. She wasn't drifting anymore.

"No, Mrs. Gerard. I'm not Patsy. I'm Sarah Ramsey. I'm Matt Ramsey's daughter."

"Such a sweet boy," she said. "Beverly had a crush on him. But we had to leave. We never came back. The police were here, you know. They talked to me. Yesterday. But it couldn't have been yesterday, could it? They came when I was a child, so it couldn't have been yesterday."

"Was the policeman's name McCarry?" Sarah asked.

"Yes. That was it. McCarry."

"Then it was yesterday. I suppose you saw the police back then, when the terrible fire happened?"

Mrs. Gerard grabbed Sarah's arm again. "They kept me away from everything. I was very young, and they kept closing doors and telling secrets. I always hated that. Children want to know what's going on."

"Yes, they do. It leaves too much to their imaginations if you don't tell them anything, and kids have good imaginations," Sarah agreed.

"And then we were never allowed to talk about it. My mother was very firm about that. No discussion ever about the fire."

Her tears were starting again. There was a box of tissues on the table. Sarah handed her one.

"You have no idea. Nobody has any idea. I did imagine what happened. I imagined terrible things. Now everything is so confused, I don't know what is true and what isn't. If Paul is here, maybe Mr. Emmet is here too," she said. "No, Mr. Emmet can't be here, he's long dead."

"Who's Paul?"

"You wouldn't like him, not after he became so strange. Mr. Emmet could be nice. But he's not to be trusted."

She was making Sarah confused. But this was an opening.

"Do you remember anything about what happened the night of the fire?" Sarah asked.

"I don't want to remember. It's not good to remember." She looked like she was about to cry again, so Sarah changed the subject even though she didn't want to.

"It must have been wonderful on the lake back then. I suppose there weren't as many cottages as there are now."

"It was getting built up. The hotel did that. People came to the hotel and liked it here and then built a cottage for themselves."

"So some of the families who have been here for generations probably started off at the hotel?" Sarah asked.

"Some of them. In its day, the hotel was quite something. Rather formal—tea in the afternoon, cocktails before dinner on the veranda, dances on the weekends."

Sarah closed her eyes and could almost see the place, the gracious people sitting on the porch sipping tea or ladies dancing in the moonlight in pretty dresses.

She wanted to hear more, but Mrs. Fraser came back and sat down and Mrs. Gerard went off into her own world again. After some polite conversation, Sarah wandered down to the dock to see the twins and the boys. She didn't stay long, and the boys left when she did.

On the way home she told them that she wanted to go to the newspaper office and see the morgue.

"The morgue. Ugh. Why do you want to go to a morgue?" asked Jake.

"It's not like for bodies. It's where the newspaper keeps its back copies and stuff. And the paper here actually has one." Sarah explained as if she had known all about it forever, not just since last week.

"How are you going to get there? It's in Milford," said Rob.

"I need a ride. I guess I could ask Jennifer to drive me. But I know she'd be too impatient to wait for me."

"My brother, Kyle, is coming up tomorrow," said Rob. "Maybe he can drive us."

"Us?"

"Sure. I'm interested in this whole thing, too. We'd better find out what it's all about before they arrest you for withholding evidence."

"That," Sarah admitted, "is a good idea." She turned to Jake. "You too? You want to come?"

"Sounds b-o-r-i-n-g," he said, dragging out the word, just like the twins did.

"Suit yourself," said Rob. "I'll ask my brother when he gets here and let you know."

Sarah thought there was a good chance he'd say yes. Rob's brother, Kyle, was a very nice guy. She had worshiped him from afar for as long as she could remember. He was never annoyed when she used to stand by his life-guard chair and he always talked to her like she was a real person, not a kid.

She couldn't wait to find out something about the names Mrs. Gerard had given her. Things could start coming together now. And the paper would have all sorts of information about the fire, wouldn't it? Three deaths. That was big news. A beautiful hotel burning to the ground. What caused it? Old stories, old news, but there were answers there. The answers were waiting for her in some yellowing old papers in a building just a few miles away.

13

Rob called Sarah early the next morning. Kyle was here and he said he'd take them into town and they would leave after lunch. They would only have a few hours, Kyle had to be back. But that should be plenty of time to go through some papers.

Little did they know.

As they drove into Milford, Kyle told them about college. It was only a twenty-minute drive into town, and Sarah was sorry when they got there. Kyle had some funny stories, mostly things like how he got lost on campus the first day and ended up in an advanced Japanese class or the feeble tricks they

played on each other in the dorm, things like that. The idea of college had not even entered Sarah's horizon. But hearing Kyle talk, it sounded like fun.

The newspaper was housed in a small brick building on a side street and the morgue was in the basement. An old man, Mr. Mills, seemed to be in charge of the morgue. He actually seemed to be in charge of a lot of things around there—he had been sweeping up when they arrived. But he was a grumpy old guy. He didn't want to be bothered catering to kids.

He led them down the basement stairs and Kyle worked his charm on him and pretty soon he was grudgingly showing them around.

There weren't any old, yellowed papers, as Sarah had imagined. Everything was on the computer or on microfilm. But the room was so dusty she wondered when the last person had been down there.

"So, what are you interested in?" Mr. Mills asked them. "What year?"

"We want 1930," Sarah said.

"What month? If this is about the Wall Street crash you need 1929."

"No, we're looking up the hotel fire on Loon Lake."

He stopped then and turned and looked at them.

"Why would you dig that up again?" he asked.

"Because of the bones that were found there," said Rob.

"What's one thing got to do with the other?" he asked peevishly.

"Maybe nothing. But now that we've heard about it, we're interested," Rob said.

"It's public information," Kyle added.

Mr. Mills grunted. "I'll get you the spools," he said and searched around on some dusty shelves. The boxes he wanted seemed to be on the top.

"Hold it, I'll go get a ladder," he said.

"No, I can reach them," said Kyle quickly. And with an easy stretch, he took down a couple of boxes, releasing clouds of dust into the air. None of them wanted to see Mr. Mills on a ladder.

But Mr. Mills had to teach them how to use the microfilm machine. And it wasn't easy. It had to be threaded with spools like an old movie projector. There was a knob that made it go fast or slow. Sometimes there were four papers on a spool, and it was necessary to search through all of them to find what you were looking for.

They were all crowded around the one machine. Kyle was operating it, but it was Sarah who knew what she was looking for.

Mr. Mills took a chair and sat by the door, tilting the chair up against the wall. He started working on a crossword puzzle.

"We need June, July, and August of 1930," Sarah said, looking for the right spools.

"How do you know it happened in the summer?" asked Kyle.

"I'm, guessing, but it makes sense. We should have asked someone the date. That was dumb, but the hotel was probably only open in the summer months," she said.

"Three people were killed. There's got to be something about it in the paper," said Rob.

Kyle had been going to leave them there and pick them up. But now he didn't say anything about leaving. He began to thread the July film.

Mr. Mills was grumbling to himself in the corner.

It took them awhile. They spooled through paper after paper on the machine. It was slow going and hard to read. And at times they got distracted with things like advertisements that offered a woman's coat for ten dollars or a man's suit for fifteen.

Then, there it was. Kyle stopped the tape. The headline was huge.

Loon Lake Hotel Burns to the Ground. Three Killed.

They were crammed together trying to read the page. It told about the blaze and about the history of the hotel and about the people who were killed.

Sarah made Kyle stop the machine at one point. The names of the three people who had been killed were listed: Raymond Steward, Emmet Harding, and Rose Bianco. A woman. Nobody had said anything about a woman being killed. Sarah remembered the twins pointing out Raymond Steward in the picture they had looked at. He was the twin's great-great-grandfather. And the name Emmet—what had Mrs. Gerard said? "Mr. Emmet was a nice person, but not to be trusted." There couldn't be too many Emmets. It was an unusual name even back then.

The article also said that Raymond Steward and Emmet Harding were the owners of the hotel. Rose Bianco, a guest, had only been eighteen years old. That got to Sarah. That was Kyle's age. That was way too young to die. Sarah hadn't been reading carefully, just skimming. Now she started to re-read all the articles, one at a time, and was really getting into it when Kyle suddenly stood up.

"We've got to go," he said. "I'm sorry. I'd like to finish this too, but everyone is getting together, kind of a party, and it's kind of in my honor. I've got to be there."

Reluctantly, they put the spools of film back in the box and Kyle hefted it onto the shelf. Sarah had wanted to read the papers that followed that one, where they would talk about the investigation of the fire and hopefully tell what had caused it and what had happened to all the people. So many questions.

Driving back, they didn't talk about college anymore. Kyle wondered aloud about what had happened to cause the fire. He asked about who owned the Big Island now, and Sarah told him that nobody seemed to know, that it had been in legal limbo all these years.

"Both partners killed. I can see why that would lead to all sorts of complications. So who's left in the Harding family?" Kyle wondered.

"I've never heard of them," Sarah said. Neither had Rob or Kyle.

"Could be Emmet Harding didn't have sons," said Kyle. "But maybe he had daughters. It would be interesting to find out, wouldn't it?"

"Mrs. Gerard would know," Sarah said. "But sometimes it's hard to talk to her."

"I think we should try," said Kyle. "I've only got two days off. I work on weekends, so I have to leave tomorrow night. Why don't we talk to her tomorrow?"

"You're going to help us?" Sarah asked, surprised. Kyle was the Brad Pitt of Loon Lake, twice as cool and popular as

Jennifer, who was way too busy for anything to do with younger kids, but here he was, offering to help.

"You have to admit, it's interesting," he said.

"What kind of job do you have, anyway?" Sarah asked him.

"Just a waiter at a restaurant. But I'm getting great tips."

"He's making a fortune," said Rob.

"There are all sorts of people who come in and that keeps it from getting dull," said Kyle, "but nothing as intriguing as what you two are involved in."

After being told she was an embarrassment by her sister, Sarah loved the idea that Kyle thought otherwise. He was such a great guy. And he was still hot as ever. Maybe she shouldn't have been so surprised when Rob showed up this summer as pretty hot himself. He had the right genes.

Kyle had some other ideas about the direction they should go in. Keep talking to Mrs. Gerard, and talk to Mrs. Fraser. Maybe there were things her grandmother had told her back when her memory was better. And then they should ask around about where Emmet Harding had lived. Did he have a family? What did anyone remember about him?

Sarah loved having a direction to go in. This was fascinating stuff. Now all she had to do was figure out what it had to do with the skeleton they found.

She absolutely couldn't wait to mention to Jennifer that she had spent the afternoon with Kyle Rearden. But she didn't get a chance.

When Jennifer came home that night, late, she stormed into their bedroom.

"Kyle Rearden?" she demanded.

Sarah kept silent and waited for her to go on.

"You went to Milford with Kyle Rearden?"

"Rob was there too," Sarah said. Her face was half hidden in her pillow. She hoped her smile didn't show in her voice.

"He's all excited about this really stupid mystery you've made up about a hotel fire a million years ago suddenly causing some dead body to appear on the Big Island."

"You don't have that exactly right," Sarah pointed out.

"Ohhh. I can't believe you," Jennifer said. "And I can't believe Kyle Rearden, either. I always thought he was so smart."

"He is," Sarah said.

Jennifer was slamming around, banging drawers and audibly throwing her clothes on the floor.

"Quiet in there," called their mother from her room.

Jennifer was reduced to noisy sighs. Not many people could do noisy sighs as well as Jennifer. Perhaps, thought Sarah, it was a special talent.

As she got into bed, Jennifer had one more shot. "You think you're so smart," she said.

"Average," Sarah replied. "Average smart."

The next day Kyle, Rob, and Sarah went over to the Frasers' cottage.

Rob introduced Kyle to the twins and they were all over him. Rob was suddenly reduced to Jake's usual invisible role.

But he didn't seem to care and Kyle was more embarrassed than flattered by their attention.

Sarah walked into the kitchen. Mrs. Fraser was sitting at the table drinking a cup of coffee.

"Can I talk to you for a minute?" she asked.

Kyle and Rob had both followed her into the kitchen. The twins had followed them. This wasn't exactly how Sarah had planned it. But she did the introduction thing with Kyle and then began.

"Mrs. Gerard mentioned some names the other day. I wonder if you know who she was talking about," Sarah started.

"Names?" said Mrs. Fraser. "Oh, you can't hold her responsible for any names. She doesn't remember things well at all."

"But still. Maybe you've heard of these people. Patsy?"

"No. I don't know any Patsy. You don't hear that name much anymore," said Mrs. Fraser.

"How about Paul?"

"Paul? There was a Paul somewhere. Let me think about that."

"Well, you must know the name Emmet Harding," Sarah said.

"Oh yes. I remember that name. He was my great-grandfather's business partner. I've seen pictures of him. He was a large man. Portly, I think they would have said back then."

"Your mother said he wasn't to be trusted," Sarah said.

"Oh dear," Mrs Fraser gave Sarah a quick look and lowered her voice. "You really can't go by anything she says. She gets so terribly confused. She might have been thinking of a movie or a book to make such a statement. That might be true for those other names you mentioned too. They might be someone she saw in a movie, or a friend from her childhood. You just never know. And, as far as Emmet Harding is concerned, he was killed in the fire too. And remember, she was only a child. She probably only remembers hearing about him."

Kyle hadn't said anything up to that point. Now he started talking to Mrs. Fraser and she fell under the spell he cast. Pretty soon he was sitting at the table having coffee with her. Sarah wondered if she was looking at a future president. She was glad to have him on her side. She figured it kept her from being such a nuisance with her questions.

"Do you think we could speak to Mrs. Gerard?" Sarah asked.

"She's napping. This whole trip has exhausted her."

"We don't want to wake her. But I thought I heard someone humming a minute ago," Rob said, nodding toward the hall.

"Maybe you could just check on her?" asked Kyle.

Mrs. Fraser was no match for the two of them.

"She's not having a great day, but I'll see," she said, getting up.

Sarah really wasn't going to push it. She liked the old lady, and as much as she wanted to ask her questions, she didn't want her crying again.

Mrs. Fraser returned a minute later.

"She wants to see you, Sarah. Just you."

Sarah followed the humming. It was some old song she knew she had heard before, but she couldn't name it.

"Mrs. Gerard?" She poked her head around the door, which was partly open.

Mrs. Gerard was sitting in a chair, looking out a small window, from which only a glimpse of the lake was visible.

"Come in, child. Come right in."

"Are you feeling well enough to talk to me?" Sarah asked, sitting down on the bed, close to her chair. This was the middle bedroom and, as in most cottages, very small.

The woman gave Sarah a little smile. "Enjoy being young," she said. "Old age isn't very much fun."

"Sometimes being young isn't fun either. Everyone can give you a bad time."

"Sarah, somehow I can't imagine you let that happen very often." She smiled again.

"I'd love you to tell me about the Big Island and the hotel," Sarah began tentatively.

"Oh, I have memories, but sometimes I feel like my brain is made out of scrambled eggs. It's up there, all my memories, but so often I can't reach them." She sighed heavily. Sarah hoped she wouldn't cry.

Not able to think of a reply to that, Sarah told her about the letter. She didn't mention where she had found it, just that she had seen a letter and now nobody believed her and it was missing. Mrs. Gerard listened very carefully, nodding now and then.

When Sarah finished, Mrs. Gerard turned and looked at her. Her eyes were very clear. Sarah knew she was definitely in this moment.

"Where did you find this letter?" she asked.

Sarah hesitated. She didn't want to upset her. But the way she was looking at her demanded the truth.

"I found it by the bones we discovered on the Big Island." Sarah held her breath after she spoke, watching to see her reaction.

Mrs. Gerard just stared into her face. Then she nodded.

"Do you know whose bones they are?" Sarah dared to ask.

She didn't answer; instead she asked Sarah a question, "What did the letter say?"

"I couldn't make out very much." She repeated the four words that she could read.

Again Mrs. Gerard nodded. She knew something. She definitely knew something.

"I want to go to the Big Island," she said.

That surprised Sarah. "Can you do that?" she asked, looking at the frail woman sitting there.

"Being old is as bad as being young. You're back to asking permission. They won't want me to go."

"I think that you know a lot about this whole thing," Sarah said.

Mrs. Gerard only smiled. She really wasn't going to admit anything.

"We're going to figure out a way, you and I," Mrs. Gerard said, and she gave Sarah a whole new kind of smile. It made her eyes crinkle.

Just then Mrs. Fraser knocked on the partly open door.

"Are you two doing all right?" she asked.

"Except that I'm hungry," said Mrs. Gerard. "Could you make me a sandwich?" This seemed to please Mrs. Fraser immensely.

As soon as she had left on her sandwich mission, Sarah asked another question.

"Do you know who Rose Bianco was?"

"I had never heard of her until the fire. She was staying at the hotel. I used to listen, you know. I listened to what people said behind the closed doors. And I heard that name a great deal. After she was killed in the fire, everyone got to know all about her. My father was killed trying to rescue her. Did you know that? I admired him terribly for his bravery. But for a long time I resented her. Why didn't she leave with the others? Why did he have to go back in after her? But then, later, I found out that she was in a wheelchair. She couldn't get out. There was no access for the disabled back then."

"How brave of him. I didn't know that," Sarah said. "What about Emmet Harding? Did he go back in because of her?"

"Nobody knows. I don't suppose anyone will ever know," she said.

"I feel there is a real story there," Sarah said, as much to herself as to Mrs. Gerard.

"Oh yes. There are stories everywhere. You are a clever youngster. You remind me so much of myself when I was young. I, too, always wanted to know the story." Mrs. Gerard was quite a hand-patter, but, somehow, Sarah didn't mind.

"We will make an arrangement, you and I," Mrs. Gerard continued. "We'll go to the Big Island. I've never been back, you know, not since the fire. But I want to go back with you."

Sarah looked at her to see whether or not she was serious. She was. If Sarah wasn't already in trouble, she was aiming toward a lot more, because she was busy trying to imagine how she would get Mrs. Gerard up that hill to where the bones had been.

Then Mrs. Fraser called from the kitchen that the sandwich was ready.

"We'll talk later," Mrs Gerard said, "but don't mention going to the island to anyone. It will be our little secret." Sarah helped her up from the chair and followed her into the kitchen.

The twins were sitting on each side of Kyle, their chairs pulled close to his. He didn't seem to notice.

Now it was Mrs. Gerard's turn to fall under Kyle's spell, and it ended up with them all eating sandwiches. Nobody seemed in a hurry to leave. What a strange situation it was. Who would have thought that Kyle Rearden would be content to sit and talk to four kids, a mother, and an old lady? He seemed perfectly comfortable. He must be practicing his skills for that future presidential campaign, thought Sarah. There could be no other explanation.

On the way home, Kyle said something very interesting, and it wasn't about being president.

"Sarah, I'm worried about your sister. She's a nice girl, and Tommy Emmerson is saying some things about her that I don't like. He's doing it just to try to give himself some points. I can't believe anyone is falling for it, but you should warn her about him."

"Like she'd listen to me about anything," Sarah said.

"She's your sister. Family. She likes the guy, she should know about what's going on."

That's all he said. And Sarah put it in the back of her mind. There was so much else going on. She should have paid more attention.

"Don't you two ever fight?" she asked the two brothers.

"What about?" Rob asked.

"Everything," she replied. She wished she had been born into the Rearden family. But an argument does take two. How much was she responsible for?

She wanted to get back to that newspaper morgue. But once Kyle left, there was nobody to drive her. Rob and Jake and Sarah had walked into Milford once to see if they could.

But it was a long dusty hike. She didn't look forward to doing it again. She would have to figure something out.

The next morning at breakfast Sarah's mother handed her a letter. It had come the day before. But Jennifer, who had collected the mail, hadn't bothered to give it to her. Sarah didn't ever get mail, except maybe a postcard from a school friend who was vacationing somewhere special. Usually, she heard from people by email.

So she was surprised when her mother handed her a real envelope. There was no return address and no stamp. Her name on the envelope was computer printed. How weird. She had a funny feeling about it, just holding it in her hand. It didn't look like an advertisement. She opened it and pulled out a single sheet of paper. It too was computer printed.

You have already been warned. Forget about the bones. Forget about the letter. Forget about all of this. Leave it alone or somebody will get hurt and maybe it won't be you, but somebody you will feel really bad about. Leave this alone. Leave all of it alone.

Sarah's mother was watching her as she read the letter. Sarah tried to be casual as she put it away in her pocket. She figured her mother didn't need any additional worries. She got up and told her mother she was meeting Rob and Jake.

Immediately, she got in her canoe and rounded up the boys and showed them the letter.

"Take this to Chief McCarry," said Rob. "He'll have to believe this."

"He'll just think I wrote it to myself," she complained.

"That's stupid. Why would you write it to yourself?" asked Jake.

"To prove I'm telling the truth about the letter."

"Oh, yeah. Did you? Write it to yourself?" asked Jake.

"Thanks a lot," said Sarah indignantly.

He looked a bit ashamed of himself, but not quite enough to satisfy Sarah. Were even her friends starting to doubt her?

"You still have to take it to the police," said Rob.

"Well," Sarah said, "That's easy. I just need to wait until the chief shows up. He's everywhere I am lately. I wonder if he thinks I'm going to murder people on the street or something."

"Maybe he's trying to protect you," suggested Rob.

"From what?" she asked.

"From the person who's writing you notes, obviously," Rob said.

She didn't know what she had expected from the boys, but they weren't being all that helpful.

They were still all together, later that day, when they went up the road to the bank of mailboxes at the turnoff from the main road. This could, at times, be a central meeting place. Everyone on this section of the lake had to walk up there to get their mail. But today nobody was there, except the chief, in his car, idling by the side of the road.

Sarah pointed him out to the boys. "I told you I'd see him sometime today."

"He gets mail, too, you know," said Rob.

"Hey, I wonder if he gets wanted posters in the mail?" Jake asked.

Nobody bothered to answer that. Sarah walked over to the car. The chief's window was open and he had his arm stretched across the sill.

"Good afternoon, little lady," he said.

Little lady? Good God.

She took the letter out of her pocket and handed it to him. He read it very slowly. She would bet he wasn't in the top reading group when he was a kid.

"Interesting," he said.

"I don't have the missing letter. But somebody does. Somebody besides us thinks there really was a letter."

Rob and Jake were approaching the car. And she wasn't supposed to tell anyone about the evidence found on the body that proved that there had been a letter.

"I haven't said anything," she told the chief in a soft voice. "Only that I saw a letter. And that was before I talked to you."

"Good," he said.

"So, what does this mean?" she asked him nodding at the note which he was still holding.

"One of a couple of things. First, you wrote this note yourself to prove something. Second, somebody's playing with you. Third, you are in some kind of danger."

"I thought a couple meant two," said Jake.

The chief just looked at him. Jake laughed. It was a nervous laugh, but the chief didn't know that.

"Let me study this," Chief McCarry said. "I'll keep it for awhile."

"I'd like to show it to my dad."

"He can come and see it anytime he wants. Is he up here now?"

"No, but he's coming back soon." Sarah actually didn't know if that was true or not, but she needed the chief to think he was.

"I'll be more than happy to talk to him anytime," said the chief. He put the letter down on the seat next to him and started to pull away.

"You watch yourself, little lady," he said. Sarah wondered how he meant that. Watch out because she was in danger, or watch out for him because she wasn't fooling him a bit?

14

That evening, after dinner, Sarah's mother handed her the phone.

"It's for you," she said. She looked puzzled.

As soon as Sarah heard the voice she realized why. She didn't usually get phone calls from adults. It was Mrs. Gerard. Her voice over the phone sounded wobbly, obviously an older person.

"Are you still game to take me to the Big Island?" she asked.

"Sure," Sarah said. Her mother was sitting across the room, not even glancing at the magazine in her lap. She was watching her daughter and listening.

"Let's do it tomorrow. Everyone here is going into Milford. I've already told them I'd rather rest at home."

This was so strange, that a grown-up had to act like a kid and sneak around to do what she wanted to.

"What time?" Sarah asked, wondering how she was going to pull this off.

"They're leaving about ten o'clock. Beverly is going to get her hair cut and the twins are going shopping. They'll be gone quite awhile."

Sarah had the brief thought that perhaps she could beg a ride with them and go visit the newspaper morgue. But no, Mrs. Gerard was more important. Once on the island, she might mention all sorts of things.

"Okay, about ten-thirty," Sarah agreed.

"Tell your mother you're coming to be with me while they're gone. That's the truth."

"Yes, it is," said Sarah, thinking it was no wonder she felt so at ease with Mrs. Gerard. Her ability to deceive was at about the ninth-grade level.

After Sarah hung up, her mother pounced.

"Who was that?" she asked.

"Mrs. Gerard, the twins' great-grandmother," Sarah said.

"What on earth did she want with you?"

"She wants me to baby-sit her while the Frasers go to Milford. I guess you don't call it babysitting, but whatever you call it."

"Oh." Her attitude changed instantly. "That's lovely of you, dear."

"Actually, I like her. She's interesting," Sarah said. She couldn't accept any credit here. She wasn't being lovely, she was being curious, as always.

Sarah was at the Frasers' at exactly ten-thirty the next morning. Mrs. Gerard must have been watching for her, because she came out of the house just as Sarah pulled the motor-boat up to the dock.

It was a little tricky helping Mrs. Gerard into the boat— she was a bit unsteady—but she had been around boats all her life and knew what to do. Sarah had intended to leave Conrad home, but he had started swimming after her, and this, after all, was all about his discovery.

"My dog really wanted to come," Sarah told her, "but if you're uncomfortable with him, I'll take him back to my house before we go to the island."

"Good heavens, no. I love dogs," Mrs. Gerard said, and gave Conrad a pat. He, of course, immediately licked her face and they both almost fell off their seats with that bit of action. This, thought Sarah, was going to be an interesting day.

She didn't think she had to be so careful about being seen. She was with an adult, and besides, if anyone was to be allowed on the Big Island, it should be Mrs. Gerard. She might even own it. And she was an old lady. Nobody could fault her for wanting to visit a place that held memories for her.

But Sarah did circle the island to see if the man's boat was there. It wasn't. She wondered if he had been back since the police had been there. She wondered if the police were watching to see if he'd come back. Or maybe they didn't believe her about the island man any more than they did about the letter.

So how would they explain the lived-in shed?

Sarah pulled up into what she now called "their cove." It was the easiest point to land.

Now she had the problem of how to get Mrs. Gerard up the hill. It had been a climb for all of them. How in the world was this old lady going to manage it?

But Mrs. Gerard surprised Sarah. When she got out of the boat, she already seemed more agile. She had worn pants and sneakers, the big, too-white kind that older people wear. Her walk was more steady in them than in the other shoes she wore.

Not that it didn't take them forever. Conrad once again led the way. They went very slowly and took a lot of rests. The ground was easier, all those police all over the island had tramped down the foliage. Conrad was in some kind of doggie ecstasy with all the new smells.

Summer had come with a vengeance since the Fourth of July, but this day was overcast and the humidity reasonable. They were walking so slowly, Sarah hadn't even raised a sweat. She commented on that.

"Ladies don't sweat," said Mrs. Gerard. "Horses sweat, men perspire, and ladies glow."

Sarah decided she liked that. She usually did a lot of glowing.

When they finally reached the hotel ruins, Sarah assumed they'd take another rest. But Mrs. Gerard was having no part of it. She stood and looked at the ruins. She was shaking slightly, but she wouldn't sit down. She didn't move a muscle. There were tears coming down her cheeks and she made no attempt to wipe them away. Sarah doubted if she even knew they were there. She wanted to say something, but she knew enough to keep her mouth shut. Her silence seemed to be exactly what Mrs. Gerard needed. Conrad understood, he sat close to the old lady and remained very still.

They stood like that for a long time. Finally Mrs. Gerard turned to Sarah.

"It was so beautiful. The building was so beautiful," she said.

"I know. I saw pictures of it," Sarah told her.

"What a terrible thing. Fire is so destructive. So destructive. Nothing is left. Absolutely nothing is left."

Now Mrs. Gerard allowed Sarah to lead her over to a fallen tree so that she could sit. Conrad followed them. He put his head in her lap.

"How could someone cause such a disaster?" asked Mrs. Gerard, absently patting Conrad. She wasn't looking at Sarah. She was staring off in the distance. Sarah wasn't even sure that Mrs. Gerard was talking to her.

"Someone caused it?" Sarah's voice was louder than she had intended.

"Such a waste," Mrs. Gerard said, as though Sarah hadn't spoken.

"Somebody started the fire?" Sarah asked again. "On purpose?" She knelt down in front of the woman, in her direct line of vision.

Even then it took a minute before Mrs. Gerard seemed aware of her.

"There are so many memories here. Do you feel them?" she asked.

Sarah wasn't sure if Mrs. Gerard was seeing her as herself or if she thought she was somebody else who would have had memories of the hotel.

"I was never on the island before this summer," Sarah told her. "I hadn't even heard about the hotel until this summer. I wish I could have seen it."

Mrs. Gerard's eyes focused again. She looked right at Sarah and Sarah knew she was back in the present.

"Let's look around," she said to Sarah.

They got up and started walking around the foundation. They came to the storage shed first.

"I don't remember this," Mrs. Gerard said as she peeked in the door. "Oh yes. I guess I do remember. It was hidden behind some rhododendron."

Then she looked at the second shed and walked over to it. This time this door was open too. They both walked in.

The bed that Sarah had seen from the window was still there, but the bedding was gone. The shelf was emptied of the books she had seen. The place had been cleaned out. Sarah wondered who did it, the police or the island guy.

The camp stove, up close, was a small and rusty old thing. There was a battered tin coffee pot on one of the two burners. The butane tank was lying on its side as though someone thought to take it with them and then didn't.

"I don't remember this building at all," Mrs. Gerard said.

"It was probably just another storage shed," Sarah suggested. "The island man made it a home, if you want to call it that."

"Island man?" Mrs. Gerard peered at Sarah over her glasses.

Sarah told her what the shed had looked like the first time she had come to the island and how a man had chased her the second time.

"How strange. I wish you had seen him. I wonder who he is? I wonder why he'd choose to be here. This is all so sad." Mrs. Gerard looked around the bare room.

"Not much of a life," Sarah agreed.

They walked again, heading across the ruins.

"I'm glad I came back here, Sarah," said Mrs. Gerard. "When you get to my age, it's the old memories that seem the clearest. I remember the hotel so well, and the fire, it was such a terrible time."

She stopped then. "Show me where." She couldn't say it.

"Where we found the bones?" Sarah asked.

"Yes. Show me where."

They walked across the foundation to the place where Conrad had made his discovery. The ground was all chopped up. It was difficult to even tell exactly where the shallow grave had been. There were footprints everywhere in the dirt, and obviously some digging had been done.

"Everything is all messed up," Sarah complained, looking around. "I'm not real sure where we found the grave anymore."

Even Conrad, sniffing everywhere, seemed confused.

"This was once a garden," Mrs. Gerard said, not seeming to care about the exact location anymore. "It was filled with beautiful roses and there was a gazebo in the middle and wrought-iron tables under the trees. Oh, such beautiful trees. It was so shady. There was a wedding right here once, right in this garden. It was lovely. I was here that day and Mother let me peek at the beautiful bride." She smiled as if she were seeing it all again.

Sarah had brought two bottles of water. She sat Mrs. Gerard down on the edge of the foundation slab and handed her one.

"So beautiful," Mrs Gerard said, still looking at the barren earth and remembering the garden. "Just beautiful. Mr. Emmet never realized that."

"Emmet Harding?" Sarah prompted.

"He was my father's business partner. Did I tell you that?" she asked.

"He was killed in the fire too," Sarah said, trying to urge her on. She sat down on the slab beside her. This was just what Sarah had been hoping for. She figured they didn't have too much time. She needed to get Mrs. Gerard back home before anyone discovered she was gone and started worrying about

her. But Mrs. Gerard didn't look like she was in any hurry and Sarah would be grateful for any little memory Mrs. Gerard would share with her.

"Yes. He was never seen again. Just like I never saw Father again. He left that morning and I never saw him again. You should get a chance to say goodbye, don't you think?"

Sarah only nodded. Mrs. Gerard was so sad. Sarah really didn't want to put her through this. She didn't want to make her think of things that made her sad. She was ashamed of herself. She started to get up. They'd go back. Sarah would forget about this whole thing. It wasn't any of her business.

But Mrs. Gerard continued to sit.

"We'll never know what really caused the fire, will we?" she asked.

"I suppose not," Sarah agreed.

"Strange though, how it all happened at the same time, isn't it?"

"What do you mean?" Sarah asked, shifting so that she could look at Mrs. Gerard's face.

Mrs. Gerard's voice took on that distant tone. Was she going to space out again?

"They were in such turmoil, Father and Mr. Emmet. I didn't understand what was happening. It was more of the listening at doors, just gathering bits and pieces. Later, when I was older, I started putting it together. There were financial problems. The Wall Street crash had happened. Everyone was frightened. Nobody could get their hands on any money. Mr. Emmet wanted to sell the hotel and he had a buyer, and my father refused. My father loved the hotel. It was his life. For Mr. Emmet it was just another investment. I might not have understood any of it at the time, but I was aware of the tension. Even a child could understand that."

"And then they were both killed," Sarah said.

"Yes. They were both killed. But was it an accident? It was as though I had been expecting something terrible to happen and then something terrible did happen. But I was a young child and nobody would even talk to me about it. They just kept closing those doors."

Sarah moved to sit on the ground in front of Mrs. Gerard, leaning toward her eagerly, absorbing the information she was getting. But then, suddenly, Mrs. Gerard turned away. She shivered.

"The past. It hovers. You'd know about that, wouldn't you, Patsy?"

"I'm Sarah, Sarah Ramsey. Who's Patsy?"

"I could have been a Sarah," she said dreamily. "Some Sallys are really Sarah. But my name is Sally, not a nickname at all."

She had come back, but not to where she had been. She didn't say another word about the hotel.

"We should go home now," Mrs. Gerard said. And she got up and started walking. She turned back to the ruins and paused for just a minute. They were standing in the shadows of the big trees. From this viewpoint the tallest chimney, rising from the rubble, looked like some kind of obelisk.

"I don't think I like this place. It frightens me. There's evil here. I feel it, don't you? I wonder if there always was." She didn't wait for an answer from Sarah.

They walked back down the hill. Sarah was careful with her. Mrs. Gerard was tired. She chatted on the boat ride back, but it was just small talk, and with the sound of the motor and her soft voice, Sarah missed most of it. Mrs. Gerard seemed content just to lean over occasionally and pat Conrad.

But Sarah was thinking about what Mrs. Gerard had said, that someone had caused the destruction. The police would have questioned everyone back then. There would be police reports, wouldn't there? Was that public information or not? There was a lot she didn't know about the way the world worked. But there was the Internet and her father. She'd find out.

They made it back before Mrs. Fraser and the twins returned and were sitting on the porch having iced tea as though they had been sitting there all day. Mrs. Fraser was absolutely thrilled that Sarah had come over to keep her mother company. The twins looked at her as if she was from outer space. In other words, thought Sarah, things were perfectly normal.

Mrs. Fraser had a cute haircut and some new highlights. She looked very pretty. Both Mrs. Gerard and Sarah commented on it.

"I like it too," said Mrs. Fraser. "It was a new stylist at Helen's. I think she's better than the one I use at home." She was very pleased with herself.

And, in a way, Sarah was pleased with herself too. She had enjoyed her day with Mrs. Gerard. There had been glimpses into the world she wanted to know about, but just glimpses. What she needed were hard facts that led to some answers. She had the feeling that she was on the verge of getting some of those answers.

15

Sarah's dad came up for the next weekend. He arrived on Thursday night and wasn't going back until Monday morning. That meant he would see the next boat race. Jake, Rob, and Sarah had been practicing. They were sure they'd win.

Thursday night and all day Friday, Sarah watched her parents carefully, with her fingers crossed. They seemed more at ease with each other. They had been spending a lot of time on the phone. Her mother was really making an effort, she put on make-up and fixed things for dinner that her dad really liked.

On Saturday he announced that he was going to see the police chief about the notes Sarah had received. He didn't want Sarah to go with him, which relieved her and at the same time made her itch with curiosity. But she asked him to ask the chief if there were any old police reports about the fire. At first he just gave her a look.

"You're staying out of this, remember?" he said.

"I know. But I can't help but be interested. Knowledge doesn't hurt, does it? I'd just like to know if the fire was caused by someone. Mrs. Gerard seems to think it might have been."

Her father finally said he'd ask the chief, just for the sake of her curiosity and her promise to stay out of it and let the police handle it.

She wasn't very satisfied when he got back. She wanted a play-by-play description of everything that had been said, complete with facial expressions. He seemed impatient.

"Well, did you at least yell at him for following me around?" she demanded.

"No. I don't yell at people," her father answered. "And he's worried about you. If you're telling the truth, then someone is threatening you. If you're not telling the truth, then he has every right to try to figure out what you're up to. I know, I know," he said with his hand stopping her before she could speak. "You *are* telling truth, but I know where he's coming from, and in a way I sympathize with him. The police deal with more people who lie to them than don't. After a while they can't help but be suspicious of everyone. And he reminded me that kids, even when caught with cookie crumbs on their face, will deny they even know where the cookie jar is."

"Did you tell him I was telling the truth?"

"Of course. I told him I knew my daughter. You don't lie."

"Did you convince him?"

"Who knows?"

Sarah wanted more. She wanted her father to be absolutely affronted that the chief would even entertain the idea that she would lie.

"Well, did you at least remember to ask about the old records of the fire?" Sarah didn't mean to sound irritated.

"I did. He said they had already checked them out. He wasn't about to share them with me. None of this is any of our business anymore. You have to get that through your head, Sarah. You need to forget about it. You have to let the police do their job."

The police could do their job, but Sarah couldn't forget about it. She was the one who had found the bones—well, Conrad, actually—and she had a personal stake in the whole thing. And how could she not be curious? It's normal to be curious. Nothing would ever be discovered if people weren't curious.

Sarah didn't exactly want her dad to make waves, but she wanted him to get Chief McCarry off her back. She wanted him to be totally on her side. There shouldn't be any doubt in anyone's mind that she was telling the truth.

At dinner that night Jennifer was in a rare good mood. She tended to behave better around their father. He didn't put up with too much attitude. But Jennifer seemed to be feeling especially good that evening. She was going to a party that night and Tommy Emmerson was picking her up. She was obviously thrilled. Sarah remembered what Kyle Rearden had said about Tommy.

"Maybe you should be a little careful of him," she ventured.

Jennifer turned to her sister, looking furious. "You're so pathetic. He obviously paid attention to you just because you are my little sister and now you're jealous."

"I'm not so sure he's to be completely trusted," Sarah said.

"Oh please. Like you'd know."

"Enough, girls." Their dad hated bickering. Jennifer had enough sense not to push it.

Conrad started barking and then they heard a knock at the kitchen door. They hadn't heard a car drive up. Jennifer jumped up and ran to open it.

Sarah couldn't believe Tommy Emmerson could arrive so quietly. He was into burning tires and screeching brakes. And she couldn't believe that he had come to the door, even if it was the back door. It was more like him to just hit the horn. But she could see that her father was pleased that Tommy had come in. They shook hands. And suddenly Tommy Emmerson was all charm. Sarah felt like gagging.

"Good luck at the race tomorrow," Tommy said to Sarah. She probed that for hidden meanings before she replied.

"Yeah, same to you."

"What happened to the hot new look?" he asked, with that half-smile on his face.

Jennifer pulled at his sleeve. "Let's go," she said. She was giving up the final pass she always gave her hair before she went out. But she wasn't about to let Tommy actually talk to her sister.

"Nice to see you, Mr. Ramsey, Mrs. Ramsey," Tommy said, shaking hands again. Then he looked at Sarah. "And you too, little one. Get some sleep tonight. You'll need it. It's going to be rough riding in my wake tomorrow." He smiled.

It was windy the next day, great for racing. The club was crowded. There must have been almost fifty people there, and Sarah's mom and dad had brought beach chairs and were right up in front. Jennifer and her friends were wandering around, socializing, not paying much attention to the boats. There had been several spills in the early races, and the wind was picking up.

Jake and his crew got a big cheer as they got into their boat, in honor of their last win. They all had smiles on their faces. But then Tommy Emmerson was suddenly beside them.

"Time for the guppies to be taught their manners," he called from his boat.

"We'll show you," answered Jake.

"Maybe you two could raise the conversation to a fifth-grade level?" laughed Rob.

Tommy gave him a look that could singe and then turned to Sarah. "How about a wager, little Ramsey?" he said.

"What kind of wager?" she asked.

"If I win, you have to get your hot look back."

"And if we win? What do I get?"

"Me?"

"Forget it."

Rob sat up in the boat. He glared at Tommy. But before he had a chance to say anything, Tommy called out. "Okay, little people. Can't let you believe you could actually beat a real sailor except as a fluke." He grabbed his paddle and guided his boat away. Hulk and Andrew Becker, that day's third crew member, were laughing.

"He's not my most favorite person," Sarah said.

"So let's beat him." Rob's voice was determined.

"Yeah. No sweat," said Jake.

It was better than a pep talk. Tommy couldn't have made them more resolved. And they started off really well. They got out in front right away. The boat was heeling over and the sails were hard to control. Sarah wanted to look back and see if she could spot Tommy, but she didn't have time, and her side of the boat was so low in the water that she couldn't see anything. Rob was having a hard time trimming the main. The wind, once it caught the sails, made the lines tear against his hands.

They were all working so hard as they approached the mark that they didn't see the boat that was passing them. Sarah looked up. It was Tommy. The worst possible sight.

It went downhill from there. They seemed to be doing everything wrong and Tommy and his crew were doing everything right. He got in the lead and stayed there. They couldn't catch up. They couldn't get a break. He was way out in front at the finish line.

After the race, after it was over and they had tethered the boat, they walked to the Beach Club yard. Last time, Tommy Emmerson had congratulated them, kind of. They needed to do the same. Sarah looked to Rob, he'd be the best spokesman.

He knew what she wanted without her saying a word. But he didn't like the idea of doing it. He knew Jake would make a mess of it, and Sarah wasn't about to do it, so he decided he was stuck with the job.

"Okay," he said "but you're both coming with me."

They walked across the lawn. Tommy was standing with Jennifer. Sarah cringed.

"Hey," said Rob to Tommy. "Good race."

"Yeah. Give you tiny tots a little wind and you can't handle it, can you?" He laughed. It was not an attractive laugh. Jennifer was looking up at his face adoringly. Sarah wanted to shake her.

"Let's see," Tommy continued, "I think that makes about a hundred wins for me, or something like that. What do you guys have? Let's count them. Oh yes, one."

"Two," said Jake. "We beat you once last year, remember?"

"Now, how could I forget that?" He put his hand to his head in mock dismay. "Let's count them again. One, two." He laughed. Sarah was starting to hate that laugh.

"Anyway, congratulations," she said and turned away. The boys were right behind her.

"What a dork," said Jake.

"First-class dork," Sarah agreed.

"I can think of some other words for him," said Rob.

Sarah's parents approached them with sympathetic expressions on their faces. Sarah had really wanted to win when her dad was watching. She geared herself for their kind words. Sometimes kind words are the hardest to take.

They said all the right things about it being a good race and what a good job they had done and that second place was still an honor. Sarah had to tune them out and look away. It was then that she noticed the man standing over by the clubhouse. She had seen him somewhere before. He was the same man who was in Peterson's store buying beer that day, when she first started noticing strangers.

"Excuse me," she interrupted her parents. "But do you know who that guy is?" She pointed at him and her parents turned to look.

"No," they both said.

The man was looking back at them. Sarah hoped he hadn't seen her pointing at him.

"Ever since we saw the island man's shack, I've been noticing strangers," Sarah said. "I don't remember ever seeing him around before this summer."

"I've never seen him before," said her mother.

"Does this have anything to do with you continuing to pursue the skeleton case?" asked her dad with a frown.

"I just wonder who he is," she answered quickly, not exactly a lie. "Maybe I should know him. Do me a favor, ask around. See if anyone knows who he is," She tried not to sound too eager.

Her dad gave her a suspicious look. Then he said, "Well, we need to go say hello to Beverly Fraser anyway. We'll ask her." Sarah's mother didn't seem thrilled with the prospect, especially after he commented on Mrs. Fraser's new haircut.

Sarah asked around too. And so did the boys. Not one person knew who the man was, and when Sarah tried to point him out one more time, she couldn't find him anymore. He had disappeared. Had it only been her imagination or had he been watching her as much as she had been watching him?

16

The next time Sarah saw Chief McCarry, she was back at Peterson's store, getting supplies for a canoe trip that the boys and the twins had planned. She was questioning how she got talked into either the trip or making sandwiches as she entered the store.

This time she was glad to see the chief. She wanted to ask him something. So she went right up to him as he was reaching for a six-pack of root beer.

"Sir," she said, avoiding using his title because she still wasn't sure what she should call him. "This time I need *your* help."

He turned immediately and gave her his full attention.

"The man I saw on the island? I keep looking for him. And I've seen a strange man around a couple of times. I could describe him for you and maybe you could get someone to draw a picture like they do on TV," Sarah said.

He laughed. "This is Mere County, not New York City or Chicago. And even if it was New York City, they only do that for suspects, not for unidentified people minding their own business."

Okay, so he thought she was stupid. She realized it did sound stupid. And now she felt stupid. He paid for his root beer and left. No help there. She shrugged her shoulders and found the things she needed. Peanut butter sandwiches weren't too difficult. Sarah was a great believer in simplicity.

The twins made a big deal out of their offerings. They had a fancy picnic basket and they were acting very coy about what was in it. The boys had brought sodas and a bag of chocolate-chip cookies.

They were headed for the White River. It was a great place to canoe, but what the twins didn't know was that you had to carry the canoe over some land to get there. Sarah was waiting to see how they'd handle that.

It took about a half an hour to get to the place where they portaged. Even though Rob's canoe was big, it was a little crowded. Rob steered from the stern, Jake paddled from the bow, and Sarah paddled from the middle seat. The twins sat on pillows on the floorboards, one in front of Sarah, one in back. They kept up a constant chatter. Usually Sarah enjoyed the quiet of the lake and the canoe's muffled progress through the water. Not this time.

Rob maneuvered the boat onto the beach.

"We're here? Where's the river?" asked Melissa.

"I don't see a river," said Megan.

"We have to portage," said Jake, getting out of the boat.

"What's portage?" asked Melissa.

"Carry," said Jake. "We have to carry the canoe to the river."

"Carry?" They both spoke at once.

"Yeah. It's light. We do it all the time," said Rob. "And with five of us it will be really easy."

"Carry?" repeated Megan.

"I don't think so," said Melissa looking at her long, red fingernails.

"We don't carry boats," said Megan.

Sarah was watching this whole thing with great enjoyment. She had already written this script in her head and they were following it precisely.

The boys were utterly bewildered.

"Well, I guess you two can carry the stuff," said Rob.

They gathered up everything. Melissa carried the picnic basket and Megan the sodas and plastic bags. When the girls were handed the paddles to carry as well, they groaned. The boys and Sarah hefted the canoe up over their heads and trudged up a small hill, across a road, and then into the woods that led to the river. It was not an easy walk. The girls, however, were dancing along, chattering as usual. Sarah heard herself grunt a couple of times as they reached another incline. In spite of Mrs. Gerard's terminology, she was sweating. The twins were not. To Sarah they looked as though they didn't have a hair out of place and their shorts and tank tops still had a crisply ironed look.

When they finally reached the river and dropped the canoe with a thud, the three of them collapsed on the ground.

"Oh, are you tired?" asked Melissa with a giggle.

"You're all wet," Megan teased Jake. "Smelly too," she held a dainty finger to her nose.

It was too bad that Sarah's glare was wasted, nobody was looking at her. And there was no comeback from the boys—they were busy catching their breaths. This hadn't worked out exactly as Sarah had imagined it.

The White River had a swift current and some serious rapids. In the early spring it was treacherous. By now it had calmed down, but there were still shoals and twists and turns to deal with. Hardly a trip went by without grounding on some hidden rocks, crashing into the bank, getting caught up in the weeds, or tipping over when the current pushed the boat.

Everyone had to wear life jackets, and the twins complained about that. But they didn't realize what was coming and Sarah was looking forward to it happening this time. She really needed to see a few hairs out of place. They could only paddle down the river with the current. They would have to be picked up at the other end.

The first part of the trip went smoothly. The twins screamed at each and every turn and this was the tranquil part. But the boys seemed to enjoy their excitement. They were very happy to keep reassuring the twins.

They aimed for their usual half-way point, a small park with a few picnic tables. It came up before they were ready for lunch, but it was the only place to stop. No one else was there, so they sat at the table nearest the river.

It was a beautiful spot, just at a bend, with rocks in the middle of the river that allowed the water to cascade over them forming white, bubbly swirls below.

The twins opened their basket. They had all sorts of salads in little plastic tubs: fruit salad, chicken salad, pasta salad, tossed salad. They even had a tablecloth, red-checked with matching red plastic plates, red paper napkins, and even red plastic spoons and forks. Sarah, Rob, and Jake had never had anything that fancy on a picnic.

Sarah was the only one who ate a peanut butter sandwich. It was smashed, as usual. She had put them in a plastic grocery bag, tied tight, like she always did. You never knew when you were going to turn over and the plastic was some protection. Soggy sandwiches were just a normal part of the trip.

Sarah actually didn't want one of her sandwiches anymore than anyone else did. She ate it out of loyalty to herself.

She was thinking how much she wished they had turned over. Their fancy salads would not have looked so good after a swim.

The boys kept commenting on the food.

"This is great," said Rob, munching on the chicken salad.

"Yeah. And deviled eggs. I love deviled eggs," said Jake. He had already eaten two.

The twins were practiced at accepting compliments. They had a special smile for them, and a small, appropriate giggle.

Sarah kept picturing the twins tumbling out of the canoe as it ran aground and turned over, and as she pictured it she wanted it to happen more and more.

They were ready to leave when someone else came to the little park. It was an old man Jake knew.

"Hi, Mr. Norton," he called. The man sat down at one of the picnic tables. He had a thermos of coffee which he opened. Then he carefully poured some into the lid of the thermos and took a sip.

"Well there," he said finally. "The Hawkins boy, isn't it?"

"Yeah," said Jake.

"And who are your friends?" he asked. He took another sip of coffee.

Jake did a clumsy job of introductions, but Mr. Norton acknowledged each of them and seemed to know both Sarah's family and Rob's.

"I don't know any Frasers," he said, as though he were failing some test.

Jake jumped right in. "Their family used to own the hotel on the Big Island," he said.

"Oooh." Mr. Norton drew the word out strangely.

That was all Sarah needed.

"Do you live on Loon Lake?" she asked.

"No, child. I live right here on the river. I always have, since I was a boy."

"Still, you must know all about the history around here," she said.

"Oh yes. I know the history. The ins and outs. The secrets and the obvious. You interested in history, young lady?"

"Lately, I am. Megan and Melissa's great-grandmother has told me a little. Her name was Sally Steward before she became Mrs. Gerard."

The twins gave Sarah one of their looks.

"The Gerards," Mr. Norton said as if confirming something in his own mind. He took another swig from his coffee cup.

"Do you know anything about the hotel and the fire on the Big Island?" Sarah asked.

"People are talking about that again, aren't they?" said Mr. Norton, but he didn't answer her question.

"Come on. Don't we need to start paddling again?" asked Melissa, obviously bored.

"Where are you girls staying?" he asked the twins.

"They're in the Carson cottage," Rob said.

"And your great-grandmother is with you?" he asked. "What about your grandparents?"

"Great-grandmother Nana is with us. Our grandparents live in Florida," Megan told him

"So, your mother is Beverly Gerard?" he asked.

"Beverly Gerard Fraser," said Melissa.

"Gets confusing, doesn't it?" Mr. Norton said. "Women should keep their maiden names. It would avoid a lot of trouble."

"Did you know Mrs. Gerard?" Sarah asked him.

"Everyone knew the Gerards," he said. "Shame when they sold their cottage."

"Maybe you could stop by and see Mrs. Gerard," Sarah suggested. "I'm sure she'd like that."

"I might just do that very thing," he said. He had finished his coffee. "I come here every nice day about this time. I have a house full of grandkids. This is my getaway place from all that ruckus."

He carefully screwed the top back on the thermos.

The twins were piling their dirty dishes into the picnic basket. Somehow the whole tablecloth, basket thing had spoiled the lunch as far as Sarah was concerned.

"It was nice meeting you, sir," said Rob, as they dumped the rest of the stuff in the garbage can.

That reminded the others to be polite too. Mr. Norton didn't seem to care one way or the other.

It wasn't until they were back on the river that Jake spoke up.

"That guy is Hulk's grandfather," he said.

Sarah and Rob couldn't have been more surprised. Hulk was massive. That old man was small and shriveled up. They didn't look related.

Sarah wondered later about the image she had allowed in her head. But it wasn't her fault. She really didn't do anything to cause what happened next.

They were in a quiet part of the river, but Sarah, Rob, and Jake knew what was ahead.

"Be careful." Rob warned the twins. "Brace yourselves. We're coming to some pretty big rapids."

"So?" said Melissa.

"Big deal," said Megan. "I'm not scared anymore. I'm getting used to this canoeing thing."

The rapids came on suddenly, just around the next bend. The current swept in from both directions and it was very hard to keep the boat going straight.

When Rob felt the first tug, he pulled his paddle close to the boat to get better control. At that point he shouted another warning, but the twins, dangling their fingers in the river, paid no attention.

Then they hit the real current.

The boys and Sarah had themselves braced. The boat should not have tipped, but Megan and Melissa were screaming and then Megan jerked up on her knees. That was all that was needed. They went over in a flash. The cold water swirled over their heads, but Sarah, Rob, and Jake immediately swam to the surface and made a lunge for the capsized boat. If it got away, it would disappear down the river. They all grabbed on at about the same time. They were fighting the current, which was trying to wrench the boat away from them. The front end suddenly gave a lurch as it caught onto a branch that jutted out into the river, which, at least, kept it from plunging farther downstream. But it was going to be hard to get it loose. It was only then that they had a minute to look for the twins. At first they could see no sign of them.

Sarah felt her heart jump. She didn't even know if they could swim, and this current was fierce. Even with life jackets, you could get tossed and turned every which way. Suddenly, Sarah was terrified for them. She called their names. She had pictured this very thing, but not like this.

The boys were shouting for them as well.

There was no answer, but finally Rob spotted them by the opposite bank, downstream several yards, clinging onto a branch for dear life. He pointed them out, and Sarah breathed a sigh of relief. She was very ashamed of herself for having pictured this very thing with relish. Something terrible could have happened. What had she been thinking?

"Stay there," Rob yelled at them. "We'll come as soon as we can."

"Hold on," shouted Jake.

The canoe, half on its side, had taken on water. They couldn't flip it back over as they did when they tipped it on purpose. Not here, not full of water. They heaved and pushed again and again.

"On three," yelled Rob. "One, two, three."

They gave it a superhuman effort and got it upright, and then almost lost it as it started to get away from them again.

Finally they had the canoe under control.

Getting into it in the middle of a roaring current was neither easy nor graceful. When Sarah made it, she lay in the bottom, which still had a few inches of water, and panted for a minute.

Jake was right behind her.

Now they had to get the boat across the river and pick up the twins, and they had to do it with no paddles. The current had probably taken them a long way down the river, most likely never to be seen again.

The fact that they were in the rapids meant that there were a lot of rocks in the river. It was shallow. Rob hadn't climbed into the boat yet. He grabbed a big dead branch and handed it to Jake, who now sat in the rear of the canoe. Jake used the limb to pushed away from the bank at the same time that Rob gave the boat a push while standing in the water. Then Rob tried to guide the boat, half standing, half swimming across, to the other bank.

Sarah untied a flotation seat cushion. It was heavy and solid and she used it as a paddle. Rob pushed with all his might. Jake poled from rock to rock, and Sarah tried desperately to keep the front end heading toward the other bank. Somehow they got it going in the right direction, fighting the pull of the current all the way.

They ended up several yards ahead of the twins. Sarah reached up, grabbed a tree branch, and held the boat steady. Rob swam back to the twins and one at a time brought them up near enough to the boat that they could grab onto Jake's stick. It took both of the boys to get them into the canoe, and with all the yanking and pulling, it took everything Sarah had to keep the boat where it was.

They were all exhausted and just sat there for a few minutes. When Sarah finally let go of the branch, they simply allowed the boat to catch the current. It twisted and turned, backward and forward, but it made its way down the rapids and down the river. There was still a lot of water in the boat, but they couldn't do anything about that until they beached it.

When they reached the quiet water, there was a collective sigh of relief from three of them. It happened at the same moment that a pitiful whine erupted from the twins. That was the first time Sarah took a good look at them. Drowned rats, or fluffy dogs after they've been bathed, or maybe featherless cartoon birds was what came to her mind. They were dripping wet, their hair hung limply in their faces, their make-up had been washed off, their clothes, skimpy as they had been, now sagged on them. Beautiful was not a word that came immediately to mind.

Jake had his mouth open again. Rob looked distressed for them. Sarah tried to keep from laughing. She tried very hard. The twins were shaking with fear and cold and misery. Sarah was also shaking, holding in her laugh. It wasn't the first time in her life she had felt an uncontrollable urge to laugh at a totally inappropriate moment.

They let the current take them at a leisurely pace down the river. Jake used his branch pole to help avoid rocks and shore. Nobody spoke, but the twins continued vaguely whimpering. When they reached their destination, they were able to get out of the canoe and drag it up onto the little beach. This place was called Parson's Point and it was where the canoe rental operation picked up their people when they completed their trips. They hauled them and the boats back to their shop. There was a phone so renters could call for their pick up. They called Jake's mother, who came and picked them up in her SUV, which had a boat carrier on its roof.

None of them had spoken. There seemed to be nothing to say. Sarah no longer found the twins' whimpering funny. Now it was just irritating.

As they waited for Jake's mom, Rob tried to soothe the twins.

"It wasn't all bad, was it? I mean, it was sure exciting for a minute."

"Exciting? Look at me," wailed Megan. "I'm a cold, wet mess."

"It was terrible. We were almost killed," said Melissa.

"I'll never set foot in another boat as long as I live," said Megan.

"We even lost our picnic basket," Melissa sobbed.

"I want to go home, real home," said Megan. Tears were running down her face. "I hate this whole place."

"We want to go back to civilization," said Melissa. "How could our mother bring us here?"

"She actually thought we'd enjoy it," said Megan. "What could she have been thinking?"

That shut Rob up. Sarah had been about to say something nice, but she didn't.

When Mrs. Hawkins came, she, too, tried to soothe the twins. But there was no appeasing them. They wallowed in their misery. Sarah was sympathetic. Wet, they didn't look like themselves. It was as though this incident had removed a piece of them, changed them, revealed them to be something other than themselves. The ride back was very uncomfortable and not just because they all were sloshing in their clothes.

And to make matters worse, Mrs. Fraser laughed when she saw them.

"Oh. This brings back memories," she said. "We used to tip over so often on the White River. Maybe I should take a river trip this summer. I really used to love it."

There was not going to be any sympathy here. The twins gave a groan and shuffled into their house.

Even Mrs. Gerard had a laugh at their expense. Sarah could hear her chortling as she opened the door for the twins.

Then Mrs. Gerard came out and walked over to the car and peered in the window.

"Sarah, my dear," she said. "You don't look any worse for wear."

"I guess I'm used to being bedraggled." Sarah said.

Mrs. Hawkins, who had left the car for a minute to have a little chat with Mrs. Fraser, got back in and they were about to leave.

But Sarah remembered something. "Mrs. Gerard, do you know a Mr. Norton?"

It wasn't exactly a double-take, but Mrs. Gerard paused and stared at Sarah.

"We met him on the river," Sarah said.

"Everybody knows Henry Norton," said Mrs. Fraser. "He's lived on the river forever."

Mrs. Gerard still hadn't said anything. She was looking at Sarah as if trying to tell her something.

"You know what," Sarah said to Mrs. Hawkins. "I'll walk from here. It's only two cottages away, and you won't have to drive down our rutted road. Thanks, though." She got out of the car.

Rob made a quick move, as if he were going to get out too, but he then he remembered his canoe was on top of the car. He sat back down.

Mrs. Gerard smiled at Sarah for having received her message.

"Enough days off," said Jake, as the car pulled away. "We need to sail tomorrow. We need to practice. We can't lose to the Duke of Dorkdom again."

"Come, bedraggled girl," said Mrs. Gerard to Sarah. "Let me get you some cookies and milk."

That sounded pretty good. Sarah followed her into the cottage.

They got a tray, took it outside, and sat at the table by the side of the house that was in the sun. Sarah had pretty much dried off, but the sun felt good.

This was a day when the lake looked almost blue. There were all sorts of boats out. They both turned and looked at the water and didn't say much for a little while.

"You said you did know Mr. Norton?" Sarah asked finally.

"Henry Norton. Of course it's Henry. He has lived on the river all his life."

"I know his grandson, Hulk. They sure don't look alike."

Mrs. Gerard was having a cup of tea and she kept taking little delicate sips. But she liked the cookies as much as Sarah did. Sarah wondered who was going to grab the last one.

Mrs. Gerard, once again, put her hand on Sarah's arm. She was a very touchy-feely person—Sarah guessed it was her way of showing affection, and she had come to enjoy it.

"Sarah, I don't know what it is about you, but I feel so much better when you're around. I think it's because you actually talk and listen to me like I'm a real person. You don't try to be careful with me and you don't jump on me when I make a mistake. In fact, I've felt really good since our little trip. I'm going to have to get out more often, whether my family likes it or not."

Sarah had to laugh. "Mrs. Gerard, an awful lot of people don't talk to me like I'm a real person either. I always thought all I had to do was get a little bit older to make that stop. I guess there's just a small window where you're a person."

"Maybe so, maybe so. Enjoy it when you get there. Now, about Henry Norton. He married a divorcee who was much younger than he was. She ran off and left him with her children. They weren't his, they were from her previous marriage. I didn't know the man well, he's a bit rough, but I so admired him for what he did. He treated those children like they were his own. Adopted them, raised them, sent them to school. He's a good man."

"That was a nice thing to do. No wonder Hulk Norton doesn't look anything like his grandfather," Sarah mused.

"Henry wasn't of my generation. He was younger. More in line with my son, a little older, I guess."

She sipped her tea silently for a few minutes. Then she spoke again.

"You know, I've been thinking about the island and the hotel and remembering those years when I was so young. They stand out in my mind because everything changed so drastically for me after that. No father, hard times. But everyone was having hard times. The Great Depression was a terrible thing. But we got through it. That's why I could never understand why my son sold the cottage. Part of me can't really forgive him for it. I never should have put it in his name. I missed out on a lot of years up here. I find myself resenting it."

"I can sure understand that," Sarah agreed.

There was only one cookie left on the plate. Mrs. Gerard went to reach for it, then looked at Sarah and didn't.

"You take it," Sarah said.

"No. It's yours. You've had the adventure today."

"I kind of told Mr. Norton to come over and say hello. I hope that's okay with you."

"That would be fine. He might help me poke my memory some more. I find I really like to talk about the old times. That's thanks to you, Sarah."

"You know, we've never talked about the Fourth of July night, when you saw the man who frightened you. He said a word. Caveat. Do you remember that? Do you know anything about a threat or a warning?"

"Oh yes. Caveat. I remember. There was a man. He looked so much like Paul. It couldn't be Paul, he'd be a very old man by now. But he was talking about a warning. He was asking me what I knew about a warning."

"That word was in the letter I saw."

"Yes. That's it. He was reading me some words. They were in a letter, he said. It wasn't making a bit of sense to me." Mrs. Gerard looked distressed. "I wish I trusted my memory more. It was a good idea you had. I'd like to talk to Henry

Norton. Let me think about it in the meantime. Let me try to unscramble my brains." She gave Sarah a weak smile.

It was time for Sarah to go. As it turned out, nobody took the last cookie.

17

The boys didn't go back over to the twins' house right away. They were afraid of what reaction they'd get for half-drowning the girls. The next few days became more like past summers. Sarah, Rob, and Jake spent one day in the canals. On another day, they tried to water ski, which they did every summer, but nobody had a powerful enough boat and it was slow water skiing, which was far more difficult than fast water skiing. They did better pulling each other on a big tire tied behind the boat. And they practiced their sailing.

Sunday they raced again. They didn't win, but neither did Tommy Emmerson. The winner was a boat that snuck up from behind at the last minute. Jake and his crew were so busy watching Tommy that they didn't see it and the same thing happened to Tommy. The *Wind Rider* came in second and the *Enterprise* came in third. To Jake, Rob, and Sarah, it was a win. They had beaten Tommy, and that was what the racing days were all about now.

But the fact that nobody was visiting the twins meant that Sarah didn't see Mrs. Gerard for a while and there were still questions she wanted to ask.

One night when Sarah got into bed, her thoughts were running rampant. It was in that little bit of time when sleep was coming but wasn't quite there yet. Sarah thought about the bones, about Mrs. Gerard, and about the life on the island in that beautiful hotel with guests dancing, having tea, and relaxing on the veranda. She saw that picture in her mind, the black-and-white one of the four people in the big wicker chairs on the porch. Suddenly, she sat up. All thoughts of sleep were gone.

There were four people in the picture, Mrs. Gerard as a seven year old, her mother, her father, and a boy who had appeared to be about eleven or twelve. The twins had identified him. It was a brother. Why had nobody mentioned him? All this talk about the family, and nobody had mentioned the brother. Was he dead? Probably. He'd be older than Mrs. Gerard. Still, it was strange that nobody had mentioned his name. Even when Mrs. Gerard was telling Sarah about the hard times after the fire, she had never mentioned a brother, only herself and her mother, and about spending some winters at the lake, and not being allowed to talk about the fire. Never a mention of a brother, at least, not to her.

She needed to speak to Mrs. Gerard. Early the next morning she went over to the twin's house. Her excuse was to find out if they were all right, to ask them if they felt better than the last time she had seen them, as if she really cared.

They were still asleep. What could be better? Mrs. Gerard was on the porch staring out at the water.

Sarah sat down next to her. For a few minutes Mrs. Gerard hardly acknowledged her, she kept gazing at the lake. Sarah hoped this wasn't one of her bad days.

Finally, she turned to Sarah. "I can't get enough of it, just looking at the lake," she said. "I've missed it so much."

"I can understand that," Sarah nodded in agreement.

Then there was another silence. Sarah couldn't wait. She just blurted out her question.

"Did you have a brother? I mean, I saw a boy in that picture with you and your parents at the hotel. The twins said it was your brother."

Mrs. Gerard turned away from the lake and finally looked at Sarah. But she didn't answer immediately.

Sarah knew enough to be a little patient, to be quiet for a moment, even though her curiosity was making her crazy.

"Paul. Paul was his name," Mrs. Gerard said.

"Paul? That's who you said you saw the night of the fireworks."

"But I couldn't have, could I? Paul would be old."

"He's still alive?"

"I don't know." Mrs. Gerard turned back to the lake for a minute, as though to gather something she needed from that peaceful view.

"You don't know if your brother is alive or not?" Sarah asked. Had she heard her right?

"We lost . . . contact," she said.

"When? Why? I mean I don't have the best relationship with my sister, but I can't imagine a time when I wouldn't know if she were alive or dead."

Mrs. Gerard smiled a sad smile. "Life is a lot more complicated than you can now imagine," she said.

Sarah sat up abruptly. That was the first time Mrs. Gerard had talked to Sarah in an adult-to-a-child kind of way. Somewhere along the line Sarah had lost her careful, respectful manners with her. She had become completely relaxed, friend to friend. That one little sentence had the effect of putting her in a different place. She didn't know how to continue and she felt uncomfortable with Mrs. Gerard for the first time.

"I'm sorry," Sarah said. "I guess it's none of my business."

Now Mrs. Gerard smiled at her. It was her old smile, a little wistful, but warm. It put Sarah right back at ease.

"You've made me your business and I like that," she said. "My brother Paul was a strange boy after the fire. It changed him. He left home after he finished high school. He contacted my mother for a few years, a card at Christmas, that sort of thing, and then we never heard from him again. It was one more great disappointment in my mother's life. That was cruel of him to do that, don't you think?"

"That was terrible," Sarah agreed.

"It was one of the reasons we never talked about the fire, I think," Mrs. Gerard said.

This didn't make any sense to Sarah. She waited to see if she'd say more.

"My brother was there, you see. He was on the island that day. There was a horse he loved over there and he had gone riding. For a while nobody could find him and my mother didn't know if he was alive or dead."

"That's horrible," said Sarah.

"I've always wondered how she got through that day, the terrible shock when she heard my father had died, and then to hear that my brother couldn't be found, and then the joy when he was found. Such up-and-down emotions. That does something to a person."

Sarah tried to imagine it, but couldn't.

"So I never blamed her for not talking about the fire. She couldn't. I could understand that, even at that young age. I've come to understand that it was the emotions. It wasn't—" she stopped.

"It wasn't what?" Sarah asked.

"Never mind," she said, and turned back to the lake.

She kept doing this to Sarah—getting right up to the point of saying something and then backing off. It was frustrating. Sarah tried a new approach.

"You know," she said. "The night of the fireworks—the man who was talking to you. I heard him—you didn't imagine it. You know it wasn't Paul. Why did you ask me not to tell? Why is it such a secret?"

Mrs. Gerard only hesitated a few seconds.

"I didn't want to appear foolish. But I'm feeling better these days. You heard him, too. I didn't imagine it. It doesn't have to be a secret, does it?"

"And that day we went to the island," Sarah continued. "I felt you had so much you could tell me. I don't like to push. But we won't ever solve anything if we don't deal with it. That day you started to tell me something. I wish you would finally tell me. You came up here when the skeleton was discovered. You must want to know about it."

"I do. I do want to know. Yet, I've been so afraid. But you're right. It's time. It's time we knew some of the answers. I'll tell you what you want to know. Just let me think about it for a little while. Let me get my thoughts in order." She sounded more sure of herself than she ever had.

The twins woke up shortly after that and Sarah had to talk to them for a few minutes. They wondered where the boys had been. Sarah told them that they felt bad about what had happened on the river.

"We forgive them," said Megan.

"Well, yes, but we'll give them a hard time for awhile about it," said Melissa with a satisfied smile.

"We've been so begging our mom to go back home," said Megan. "And Dad's on our side. He wants us back there."

Sarah definitely had mixed emotions about that news. The girls could leave as far as she was concerned, but she wanted Mrs. Gerard to stay, and both things couldn't happen.

It was almost the end of July, and Sarah's father was talking about coming up for two weeks at the end of the summer, after all. Sarah's mother seemed both pleased and anxious about this news.

Sarah caught her one day in front of the full-length mirror in the cottage. She was looking at herself intently.

"My hair, when did it get to be this much of a mess?" Jean Ramsey asked her daughter.

"It's fine," Sarah said, although it did look a little straggly. But she was Mom and she was fine.

"No, it's not fine," her mother said, and pulled at a piece that fell on her forehead. "Maybe a haircut, then," Sarah suggested. "You should go to the woman Mrs. Fraser went to in Milford. She says she likes her better than the one she uses at home."

"She got that cute cut in Milford?" asked her mother.

"Yeah, the day . . ." Whoops, she almost said the day she went to the island with Mrs. Gerard. "The day I was with the twin's Nana," she revised quickly.

"Maybe I'll call her for the name," said her mother. She went over to the phone and picked it up, but she still hadn't dialed when Sarah went outside with Conrad. Her mother hadn't seen much of Mrs. Fraser since her dad had left.

Strange. It was uncomfortable when parents acted like middle-school kids. They were supposed to be above all that.

Jean Ramsey did make an appointment, for the next morning. She told Sarah at dinner that night.

"I want to go with you," Sarah said immediately.

"You do?" Her mother was surprised. "You want your hair cut?"

"No. I just want to go into Milford."

"You usually accompany me kicking and screaming. You hate to be away from the lake," she said.

Sarah shrugged. "I feel like going, okay? And maybe Rob and Jake will want to go too."

Her mother looked at her strangely. Sarah was getting used to those looks.

She rounded the boys up right after dinner. Two phone calls and then they met in the middle of the lake. Two canoes and one kayak. All the kids did that sometimes, even the older ones, forming a circle in the middle of the lake by clinging to each other's boats with one hand. This night, the lake was quiet, only some float boats out, the ones adults like to cruise around in at dinner time, their cocktail cruises.

Sarah asked them to go with her to Milford the next day, to look up more stuff in the newspapers. At first Jake balked at the idea.

"We should be sailing," he insisted. "Not that many races left."

"We need your help," Rob told Jake.

"Come on. We won't have all the time in the world and there's so much to go through. Don't you want to see what a morgue looks like?" Sarah asked him.

"Not that kind of a morgue," Jake said. "Maybe the other kind, or maybe not."

"The other kind would gross you out," Sarah teased.

He never actually agreed to go, but he was in the car when they left for Milford the next day.

Sarah's mother parked in front of the beauty salon.

"Give me about two and a half hours," she said. "I'm going to have a manicure and a pedicure, as well, and then I might even go into Lilly's Dress Shop." She offered to buy them lunch afterward at the diner.

"If we're not there, go ahead and eat without us," Sarah told her.

She gave her daughter another one of those looks.

"I'll be there," said Jake. "Double-chocolate hot fudge sundae. Are you kidding?"

They waited until she walked into the salon before they hurried toward the newspaper office.

They knew where to go this time. They ran down the basement stairs. Mr. Mills was there in his chair, leaning against the wall in much the same position as they had left him. But this time his greeting was altogether different.

"Hi there," he said.

Both Rob and Sarah were surprised. He had been so crabby the last time. But he wasn't looking at them.

"Good to see you Jake," he continued. "Been a long time. I sure miss your granddad. Don't see any of the old fellows anymore since he's gone. We don't even get together to play cards anymore."

"Hi, Mr. Mills," said Jake. "Yeah. I miss him too."

"Great fellow, your granddad. So, what can I do for you kids?"

"We're here to look at the same microfilm we wanted before," Sarah said. "We didn't have time to finish."

"We know where to find it," said Rob. "We won't have to bother you."

"No bother at all," said Mr. Mills. He got up from his chair and led them back to the same aisle as before. "I remember, 1930, wasn't it? Old brain's still working."

Rob dragged the box down and carried it over to the microfilm machine. This time, Mr. Mills produced a rag and wiped off the box. He even gave the chairs a swipe.

"You kids so interested in history, that's a good thing. Your granddad used to have some stories, didn't he, Jake? Great storyteller, that man. Probably what gave you an interest in the old times."

"Yeah, he always had a story," said Jake. "If he were here now, I'm sure he'd tell us stuff about the fire on the Big Island. Before his time, I guess, but he'd know about it."

"Everybody knows about it. Talked about it for years," said Mr. Mills. "I guess they're still talking about it. A man came in here not too long ago and looked at the very files you're looking at."

"Who? When?" Sarah asked quickly.

"Don't much remember a name, not sure he ever gave one," said Mr. Mills. "Nice looking fellow. As to when, I guess it was in the spring, before the summer folks came back. That man sure took a lot of notes."

"How old was he?" asked Rob eagerly.

"Hard to say. Everyone looks young to me anymore. My guess would be forty or so."

They tried a few more questions, but Mr. Mills hadn't paid any more attention to the man than he had to them on their first visit. They settled down at the machine.

They wanted to continue from where they left off, but it was difficult and they had to plow through the same spools again. Running the machine hadn't become any easier. They would go too fast and miss things, or too slow and see a lot of things that didn't interest them.

"Here's something," Jake said, stopping Sarah's hand on the knob.

There was a headline on the second page:

Minor Suspect in Arson

No name was given, withheld because of age, but a young boy with a previous history of starting fires was at the scene at the time. The article said the police were investigating.

"That's interesting," said Sarah.

They searched for what came after that, but there didn't seem to be anything more about the boy. There was an editorial that wondered if the motive for the fire might have been insurance.

"Did they have fire insurance back then?" Sarah asked.

"Sure they did," said Mr. Mills. He had been standing behind them, looking at the articles with them. "Insurance has been around for a long time. People have been up to the same tricks for a long time too. There were a lot of fires back then, right after the crash. Businesses failing, then suddenly catching on fire and getting insurance for the building. Saved more than a few people in financial trouble. Except some of the insurance companies failed about then, too."

"That could be the motive," Sarah said.

"Could be," said Rob. "But who would have gained from it? Both partners in the hotel were dead." They went back to their reading.

As it turned out, the thing that caught Sarah's attention wasn't about the fire at all. She had already skimmed several headlines concerning the subject, but this one caught her eye.

Senator Wants to Repeal Prohibition

"Wait a minute," she said. "Prohibition was still going on in 1930?"

"Sure it was," said Mr. Mills. "It ended in 1933."

"So what?" asked Jake.

"Maybe I owe Mrs. Dill, my history teacher, an apology. I've done plenty of complaining about 'Dill's Dull Dates,' but maybe dates are important after all," said Sarah.

"What are you talking about?" Rob asked.

"Something's not right here," Sarah said. "But let me think about it. I don't want to say anything just yet." She looked at Mr. Mills sitting there listening intently. Rob got her message. Jake didn't.

"Why the big mysterious act?" he asked.

"Let it go for now," said Rob. "Sometimes you have to actually think about things before you spit them out."

Jake didn't get that either.

Their two and a half hours had gone quickly. They put away the box and thanked Mr. Mills, then met Sarah's mom, who was waiting for them in front of the diner.

"Whoa, Mrs. Ramsey," said Jake when he saw her. "Cool 'do.'"

Jean Ramsey smiled and patted her hair. It was cut shorter than she usually wore it, capping her head in a way that made it swing when she moved. She was very pleased with herself.

They all celebrated with especially demonic desserts after their sandwiches. Sarah felt they had really accomplished something that day, and she couldn't wait to share her suspicions with Mrs. Gerard.

18

The next day, when the boys and Sarah swam out to her raft, and they were sitting there talking, Sarah told them about going to the island with Mrs. Gerard. They were speaking in low voices, so the sound wouldn't carry to the fishing boats nearby. She cautioned them not to tell anyone else.

And she told them about what she had been thinking.

"Nineteen-thirty. Prohibition was still going on. Yet Mrs. Gerard, when she was talking about the hotel, told me about people having cocktails on the veranda in the evening, and I saw it myself in that picture the twins showed me. So, maybe it was apple juice or something, but I don't think so. There were people in the background of that picture and they definitely had cocktail glasses in their hands."

"Bootleggers? Are we talking about bootleggers?" Rob asked excitedly.

"I don't know, drinking was illegal, but by 1930 Prohibition was on its way out. People were tired of it. What better place than an island to go and be able to have a drink before dinner? In a way, it could have been a selling point for the hotel."

"So the bones belong to a bootlegger or a Fed?" asked Jake equally excited.

"I don't know. Maybe an insurance investigator. That would make sense, too," Sarah said.

"Yeah, that would make a lot of sense. But who was there left to kill the guy? The two partners were already dead," Rob said.

"We don't know if the bones were there before or after the fire," Sarah pointed out.

"Yeah, but, yeah, but—you might really be on to something," said Jake, his voice rising in excitement. "I mean, we're talking about the age of gangsters, Al Capone, bank robbers, and stuff. Maybe that's what this is all about. Gangsters shooting each other."

"On Loon Lake?" asked Rob. "That's hard to believe."

"But what about now?" asked Jake. "All that happened a long time ago. What about those notes you got, Ramsey? They were threats. Who would care about any of this stuff now?"

"That's the question, isn't it?" Sarah agreed. "Somebody doesn't want anyone to know who those bones belonged to. Why would it matter now?"

"There's a lot we don't know," Jake admitted.

"Yes, there is. But Mrs. Gerard knows. Somehow we have to make her remember," Sarah said.

"But she's a wing-nut," said Jake, exasperated.

"Sometimes her brain gets a little confused," Sarah said. "But mostly she's really with it."

"Let's go talk to her," said Rob, standing up.

They all dove into the water and swam back to shore. They had left their clothes lying on the dock, and they toweled themselves off enough to put them on over their suits. Sarah had to put Conrad in the house—he liked to lie on the shore like some kind of lifeguard when they were out on the raft. But he didn't protest being left behind. He must have been ready for his afternoon nap. They got into Rob's canoe and went right over to the Fraser place. This time, Sarah didn't even pretend to be visiting the twins. Mrs. Gerard was sitting on the porch and seemed glad to see them.

When the twins came bounding out, they were a bit surprised when Rob said, "We want to talk to your great-grandmother for a few minutes."

"What about?" Melissa demanded.

"Well, we're still mad at you, anyway," said Megan, with a pout.

"Oh yeah, the canoe trip. We're sorry about that. We didn't mean for it to turn out that way," Rob told them, but then he turned his attention back to Mrs. Gerard.

Sarah should have been elated. But somehow she felt sorry for the twins. No time to dwell on that. They had important business here. They kept to small talk until the twins got tired of the whole thing and wandered away.

Then they looked at each other to see who would start.

"Mrs. Gerard," said Rob. "We want to know what life was like when you were growing up here."

"You want to know if I know anything about the bones," said Mrs. Gerard. She was definitely feeling sharp today.

"Well, yes, especially that. But it must have been pretty interesting living back then, with the Wall Street Crash, the gangsters, Prohibition, flappers, and everything," Sarah said.

"I was way too young to be a flapper and I wasn't even aware of any of those other things," she said. Yet she had a smile on her face, as if she were remembering something.

"But about the fire, the old newspaper mentioned something about insurance, that maybe that was a motive. Was the hotel insured? Did your family get any money from it?" Sarah asked.

Mrs. Gerard looked puzzled at the question. "They couldn't have," she said slowly. "We went through such hard times."

"But they ended, the hard times?" Jake asked.

"Yes, yes, they did. My mother was an amazing woman. There weren't many single mothers around back then, like there are now. But my mother, as a widow, would have fit into that category. She was, however, a determined woman. After two winters up here, we went back to the city. She had found out about another investment my father had with Mr. Emmet. It was a small restaurant. She took it over and made quite a success of it." She still had that puzzled look on her face.

"Insurance . . ." Mrs. Gerard repeated, her voice trailing off.

"You remember something?" Sarah prodded.

"The box," she said suddenly. "I had forgotten all about the box." A look of joy came over her face. Then it darkened again. "But it would be long gone by now, wouldn't it? That's one reason why I was so upset when my son sold the cottage. I never got a chance to go back for the box. He just announced one day that it was sold and we never went back. I can't believe I had forgotten about that."

"What was in the box?" Rob asked.

"It was my mother's box. There were papers in it. But when you asked about insurance, that made me remember it. There were insurance papers in there. My mother explained that to me. It was a year or two after the fire. She was worried all the time, and she had me hide the box. She said maybe someday I would need it, but not to touch it until she was long gone. I always thought that was a strange thing to say."

"So you hid the box? Where?" Sarah asked.

"At my cottage. The one that was sold," she said simply.

"Where in the cottage?" asked Jake.

Mrs. Gerard smiled then. "I was very shy back when I was a child. I had a place where I went when I wanted to get away. And after the fire, I wanted to get away quite often. My brother, Paul, wasn't very nice to me sometimes. I hid the box in my place. My mother told me to hide it there. She never minded me going there. Nobody minded after my father died."

"Where was this place?" asked Jake, a bit impatiently.

Mrs. Gerard just looked at him, not approving of his tone of voice.

"We have a place too," Sarah said quickly, to get things back on an even keel. "It's up on top of the big hill. We built a tree house up there. I think every kid needs a place."

Mrs. Gerard smiled again. "Mine was under the porch. There was a crawl space under there. My father had forbidden me to go there. He said there were snakes and, besides, I always got dirty. But my mother understood. She knew I went there and she didn't ever say anything. I never saw a snake."

"Where was your cottage?" asked Rob.

"Why around the cove, of course. I thought everyone knew where the Steward cottage was. It was still being called the Steward cottage when my son sold it to the Emmersons."

"The Emmersons?" The three of them said at once.

"I'm sure that's the name. I'm sure because Louise Harding married a man named Robert Emmerson. And Louise Harding was the daughter of Michael Harding who was Emmet's son. I'd hardly forget anything about that family."

"The Emmersons?" Sarah repeated.

"The Emmerson family is descended from Emmet Harding, your father's partner?" asked Rob.

"Yes, of course. I would have thought you knew that. Or maybe it was just in my day that we spent so much time worrying about where people came from and who they came from. Nowadays nobody cares about things like that."

"Tommy Emmerson's great-great-grandfather was Emmet Harding." Sarah said it out loud, although she was really just trying to get her brain around this very interesting new fact. "And you stayed in touch with that family?"

"They kept coming back to the lake. They rented from different people until our cottage went on sale."

"Why wouldn't it still be there?" asked Jake.

Everyone turned and looked at him.

"The box. Why wouldn't it still be there? Who would have been looking around in a crawl space under a porch?"

"It probably *is* still there," agreed Rob.

"Do you think so?" said Mrs. Gerard eagerly.

"Maybe." Sarah didn't want to get her hopes up.

"We need to go and look," said Jake.

"What? We knock on the door and ask if we can look around under their porch?" Sarah asked.

"Oh, heavens, no," said Mrs. Gerard. "They must not know about the box, if they haven't already found it, and they must not know. And I don't think they have found it because nobody has claimed . . ." Her voice drifted off.

"We can go now," said Jake. "Tommy's out of town anyway. He's not even racing this Sunday. Probably not next Sunday either."

"He's gone?" Sarah asked. "Where did he go?"

"Something to do with the campaign?" asked Rob.

"I suppose so," said Jake.

"What campaign? What are you talking about?" Sarah asked, looking from one to the other.

"Tommy's father is running for State Attorney General," said Rob.

"Mr. Emmerson's got an eye on being governor," said Jake. "At least that's what my dad says."

Sarah never paid attention to what anyone's parents were doing. She hadn't been aware of any of this. How come the boys seemed to know all about it?

"Interesting," said Mrs. Gerard. "Emmet Harding had political ambitions too. Must run in the family. I believe Michael served a couple of terms in a state congress somewhere."

"So nobody's home at the Emmerson place?" Sarah asked.

"I'm not sure about that, but we could check," said Rob.

"Now, don't you children do anything dangerous," said Mrs. Gerard. She sounded both concerned and excited.

"Where under the porch would we find the box?" asked Rob, ever-practical.

Mrs. Gerard closed her eyes, obviously trying to remember. Finally she spoke. "I went in on the side toward the foot of the lake. There were some loose boards there. Then I went to the back, where there was a log. I dug a hole under the log and I hid the box in the hole. It won't be easy to find. It's very dark in there. I think I was about ten years old when I hid the box. I didn't go in there much after that. I was getting too big and I guess I didn't need it anymore. I only went there before I realized I didn't have to hide, all I had to do was look at the lake to feel calm when I was unhappy about anything." She stared right at Sarah as she said that last part, and she smiled.

There was one more subject Sarah wanted to bring up with Mrs. Gerard, but she didn't know quite how to approach it.

"You said your brother wasn't very nice to you. What did you mean by that?"

Mrs. Gerard looked at Sarah, studying her. "I was raised in an era when you didn't tell tales out of school. You didn't air dirty linen in public. Family business was family business. People are much more open and honest nowadays."

"Yeah," said Jake. "My grandfather used to tell me about that. He said people didn't even talk about disease, like having cancer was shameful or something."

"That's true," agreed Mrs. Gerard.

"I didn't mean to pry," Sarah said defensively.

"I know you didn't, my dear. But it's odd for me to talk about it. Yet, I feel better after I do. Secrets aren't healthy."

Mrs. Gerard was being open and honest. Sarah stopped trying to go around the subject she wanted to talk about. "When we were reading the about the fire, an article mentioned that a minor was a suspect in starting the fire."

"It was in the papers? I never knew that," said Mrs. Gerard. "I was only seven. There was so much I didn't understand. But my brother had started a fire once. He liked to play with matches and got in trouble for it. And one time he and his friend tried smoking a cigarette out by the old shed and it caught on fire. It was Paul who had the matches and so he was blamed. Then, when the Big Island fire happened, he was there, so he was a suspect. That's a big reason my mother would never talk about the fire. It upset Paul horribly to have it mentioned. He became a different person after all that. He couldn't stand that people suspected him. I'm sure that's why he left after high school. He just wanted to get away from that suspicion. I'm sure that's why he never came back."

"Wow," said Jake. "I've been accused of stuff I didn't do, too. Nothing that big, but even little things are hard to take."

"We're going to get you that box," said Rob with some forcefulness.

"Don't get yourselves in any trouble. Maybe I shouldn't have said anything," said Mrs. Gerard. "If you got in trouble, I'd never forgive myself."

"We won't get in any trouble," Jake said confidently.

Sarah wasn't so sure. She was learning that things didn't always turn out the way you expected.

Just as they were leaving, Mrs. Gerard happened to mention one more thing.

"The other boy, Paul's friend, was the Harding boy. I was never convinced that he hadn't started the shed fire and let Paul take the blame. He was that kind of boy."

"There was a Harding boy?" Sarah asked.

"Yes. I told you. Michael Harding. Louise Harding was his daughter and she married a man named Emmerson," Mrs. Gerard explained, a bit impatiently.

"Was Michael Harding on the island when the big fire happened?" Sarah asked.

"It was never mentioned, at least not to me," said Mrs. Gerard.

"And Michael Harding and your brother, Paul, were friends?" asked Rob.

"They spent time together, but I'm not sure they ever really liked each other. They fought a lot," Mrs. Gerard said with a small frown.

So many details coming out, so many people involved in one way or another, and it was so long ago. They'd all be dead or very old. But it was becoming real in Sarah's imagination. She was beginning to see it like a play, the characters moving around a stage, assuming their various roles. So who was the villain and who the hero, and was one of them a murderer?

19

They went over to the Emmerson/Gerard/Steward cottage that very afternoon. They had their story all ready—they needed to talk to Tommy about the races, even though they knew Tommy wasn't going to be there. But maybe his mom or someone was there.

It was obvious that no one was home: the shutters were closed and the porch furniture was under tarps.

They would have tried for the box right then, but the people next door were out on their dock.

"Nobody's home," a man called over.

"Looks like it," said Rob. "We'll come back later. Know when they'll be back?"

"Couple of weeks," the man said.

They returned to their boat, trying to look disappointed. But it couldn't have been better. Now they knew they would have plenty of time to look for the box.

Except, of course, they couldn't wait.

That very night, after dark, Rob picked up the other two in his canoe. They traveled silently through the water, paddling carefully so they didn't even make a splash.

At a lake, people are outside all times of day and night, just looking at the stars, gathering around a campfire, or taking a midnight dip. But the house next door was dark. And the cottage on the other side was around a bend. They were in luck.

They pulled the canoe onto the shore and quietly made their way up to the house. It was so dark they couldn't see where they were walking. They had brought flashlights, but they didn't want to use them until they absolutely had to. Sarah bumped into Rob at one point. But still, they were silent. They felt their way around the house until they were at the side facing the foot of the lake. This side was away from the near neighbors. They dared one flashlight.

The latticework that covered the crawl space had been recently painted. That wasn't good. And sure enough, they couldn't find any loose slats, but the slats were thin, more decorative than useful. They managed to pry off a couple. It wasn't easy to do it without breaking them. Rob had a pocket knife and he was able to wiggle the small nails loose.

Finally, they had a little space opened. Sarah crawled in and so did Jake. Rob was still struggling to wedge himself in when Sarah started creeping toward the back. Now she felt free to use her flashlight. The ground was hardened dirt. It felt wet to the touch. She wasn't convinced that there weren't any snakes.

Jake was right behind her.

"Can you see a log?" he asked. He was flashing his light all over, bouncing the light on the floor, the walls, and the ceiling.

The beam from Sarah's light was too focused, she could only see a small spot at a time. When Mrs. Gerard had talked about a log, she had imagined something big. There was nothing like that.

Jake was wiggling himself toward the back of the crawl space. Rob was trying to pry off more nails, Sarah could hear the squeak of the wood being pulled away. Those new shoulders were causing him some trouble when it came to squeezing into small places.

"I see something," Jake said in a loud whisper.

Sarah crawled toward his voice. Sure enough, there was a small log, only about six inches in diameter. They pushed it aside. It was a long, though—where should they start digging?

They had brought garden trowels with them. Sarah started to dig at one end and Jake started at the other.

"This place probably flooded a couple of times in all these years," Sarah said "This log could have moved a long way from where it started."

"I don't need to hear that right now," Jake told her.

"Keep digging."

Sarah was making a little ditch with her trowel that extended about a half a foot on each side of where the log had been. It was taking her a while, but she and Jake were getting closer together as they dug. All Sarah was finding were worms and bugs.

"Shut off your lights, someone's coming," Rob whispered hoarsely from outside.

They both switched off their flashlights and there was complete darkness. Sarah literally couldn't see her own hand. It was hard to believe little Sally Steward hid under in this place and found it comfortable.

"Who are you and what are you doing here?" called a voice from outside.

"Just me," Rob called back.

Sarah and Jake crawled over, peered through the slats, and saw a flashlight beam. It was lighting up Rob's face. Rob had turned his light off, so they couldn't see the man who was talking.

"And who is 'me'? Hey, you're the kid who was here this afternoon. What's your name?" The voice was cross and accusatory.

"John Jones . . . ton," Rob said, his voice faltering.

Rob Rearden telling a lie? Sarah was surprised, but grateful. And, after all, Mrs. Gerard didn't want them getting into any trouble.

"What are you doing here? I told you nobody was home."

"But. Tommy said he'd leave me something. I was to come over and get it. I was looking around. Maybe he left it by the porch?"

"Leave you what?" The voice didn't sound the least bit convinced.

"A paper and—a key. It's important. I have to have it before tomorrow. I know he must have left it. He knew how important it was." To Sarah, it was obvious that he was making it up as he went along. Hopefully, it sounded better to the man.

"Key to what?" asked the man.

"It's—confidential," said Rob.

Sarah was surprised how good he was at this lying stuff.

"I can call them, you know," said the man.

"Hey, that's great. Do you have the number? That would be great."

The man didn't answer. How did Rob know to call his bluff? Sarah knew she would have been running for the woods at that point.

"Never mind. Just get out of here. I'm watching things for them and I don't want to see you stalking around here late at night." He turned and walked away. Rob was silent for a few minutes and so were Sarah and Jake.

"Let's get out of here," Rob said in a low voice.

"We've only got a few feet to go. You walk toward the boat and leave. Meet us just past the bend," Sarah told him.

She heard him walk away. Then she turned her flashlight back on and continued to dig.

"Jeez," whispered Jake. "That was scary."

"Yeah," Sarah agreed. They were both digging furiously.

"Rob's a good liar," said Jake.

"We need to remember that in case he ever pulls it on us."

"Whoa," said Jake, excited. "I hit something."

Sarah scrambled over and helped him dig. They pulled out a dirt-covered metal box about the size of something you'd get with a dozen doughnuts.

"We found it," he said, too loud.

"Shhh," Sarah warned. "That neighbor might be listening."

Cautiously, they crept back over to where they had come in. Rob had replaced the boards, that's why the man hadn't noticed the gap. But they weren't nailed in. It was easy to shove them aside and twist their way back out. They had already turned their lights out. They stopped and listened before they made their way into the woods, and they walked until they came to the heavy brush before they turned their flashlights back on. They were away from the Emmerson property by that time. The neighbor couldn't stop them from walking in the woods.

Rob sat in his canoe, waiting for them, just on the other side of the bend. Jake shone his light on the box to show him they had it, but none of them spoke. They got into the boat and silently paddled away. Indian paddling was something they had spent a great deal of time on when they were younger; their paddles went in and out of the water without a splash.

It wasn't until they pulled up to Sarah's dock and walked up to her porch that they got a good look at the box.

Sarah's mother had the TV on inside the cottage–she hadn't even heard them come on the porch. They all crowded around the table where Rob had put the box down.

It was a metal box, covered with dirt and was, of course, locked, but also probably rusted shut.

"Hurry up, open it," said Jake in a low voice. None of them wanted to disturb Sarah's mother and be interrupted.

"We'll have to pry it open," Sarah said.

"No. We can't open it," said Rob. "It's Mrs. Gerard's box. She should open it, or give us permission."

"You're no fun," said Jake. "Besides, she doesn't know what condition it's in. We can pry it open and tell her we found it like that."

"No, we can't," said Rob.

"Like you can't tell a lie?" Sarah teased. "You actually seemed pretty good at it back at the cottage."

"Besides, she's just an old lady. She'll never know," said Jake.

Sarah felt herself bristle. "She is *not* just an old lady."

"No, she's not. She deserves our respect," said Rob.

"What time is it?" Sarah asked, then looked at her own watch. It was almost eleven o'clock. "It's way too late to go over right now, isn't it?"

"Yeah," said Jake. "Old people go to bed early."

Rob handed Sarah the box. "You keep it. I'll be over early tomorrow morning and we'll take it to her."

"I want to see it now," insisted Jake. "Maybe there's something really gross in there."

"There's nothing gross, " Sarah told him. "It was Mrs. Gerard's mother's box."

"There probably isn't even anything interesting. I bet it's business papers and things like that," said Rob.

"So what time can we go over in the morning?" Sarah asked.

"Old people get up early," said Jake.

"So speaks our resident geriatric expert," said Sarah. "But he's probably right."

"Let's say nine o'clock. I guess it wouldn't be polite to go before that," said Rob.

They all agreed reluctantly. They had gone to a lot of trouble to get this thing, and now they had to wait to open it.

When Rob and Jake left, Sarah took the box and put it under the bunk beds. It gave off a moldy, earthy odor that fascinated Conrad. Would Jennifer complain and try to find out what smelled? Or did Sarah notice it only because she knew it was there? Of course, Jennifer wasn't around anyway. Sarah sat and watched TV with her mother for awhile. But she wasn't thinking of the really dumb game show she was watching–she was picturing various ways to get that box open.

She was already in bed when Jennifer came home.

"Sarah, your sneakers stink," she said. "Don't you ever wash your feet?"

"Go to bed," Sarah told her, glad to accept the blame for stinky feet, just so Jennifer didn't scrounge around and find the box. But she had smelled it, too. All those years in the ground had left their trace.

The next morning Sarah was on her dock a few minutes before nine. Rob pulled up with Jake just after she got there. They paddled over to the twins' cottage.

The girls wouldn't be up yet, but Mrs. Gerard was sitting on the porch with a cup in her hand. She stood up as they tied the canoe to the dock. Sarah waved the box at her.

She was holding open the porch door for them as they walked across the lawn. Excitement shone in her eyes.

"Is anyone else up?" Sarah asked her.

"Beverly is up and out. She likes to take the rowboat out in the early morning." Mrs. Gerard's hands were quivering as she reached for the box.

"It's pretty dirty," Sarah told her. Rob gathered a want-ad page from a city paper that was lying on the sofa and put it on the table, and Sarah put the box on top of that.

"We didn't open it," announced Jake, as though he had been responsible for the restraint.

Rob gave him a look as they all gathered around the table.

"Do you have a key?" Rob asked Mrs. Gerard.

"I did once," she said.

"It probably wouldn't matter, I'm sure it's rusted shut," he said. "We'll have to pry it open. I brought this." He held up a screw driver.

"Please. Open it," said Mrs. Gerard. She was hardly able to contain herself.

Rob worked the screwdriver, trying to wedge it between the top and the bottom. Rust was coming off in flakes and getting all over his hands and his forearms. Jake reached over and held the box, and his hands instantly turned orange.

"Messy work," said Mrs. Gerard. "I hope you didn't have any difficulty getting it."

"No, no." Sarah said quickly.

Finally there was a popping sound and the top gave way, coming off in Rob's hands. They all looked inside the box.

"That's all?" said Jake, disappointed. "Just a bunch of papers?"

"That's all," said Mrs. Gerard. But her voice was full of eagerness. She reached for the papers. Rob took them out and handed them to her. He wrapped up the box in the newspaper and took it out back to put in the garbage.

Mrs. Gerard stood and stared at the papers in her hands. Then she looked at Sarah.

"I know you're curious. And you went to all the trouble to get the box for me. But would you mind terribly if I look through these alone? There are memories in here."

Sarah's disappointment showed on her face.

"I'll share the information with you, I promise, especially if there is anything pertaining to the fire and the island. Tit for tat, as we used to say."

"Sure," Sarah said. What else could she say?

Jake headed for the door, head down.

They met Rob coming from the back of the cottage and they walked dejectedly to the canoe.

Jake told Rob what Mrs. Gerard had said. "We went to a lot of trouble for nothing."

"It's not for nothing," Sarah said. "She'll keep her promise."

"Maybe. Maybe not, if there's something incriminating," said Rob.

"She was only seven years old," Sarah said.

"Not her, her family. If her family did something wrong, I can't see her letting us know about it," said Rob.

"Like start the fire on purpose?" asked Jake, his interest renewed.

"Like, anything," said Rob.

"I feel like someone offered me a piece of candy and then pulled the box away," said Sarah. "We're so close to getting some answers and now we have to wait some more. I really hate waiting."

20

That Sunday Jake, Rob, and Sarah won another race. But Tommy Emmerson wasn't there, so it didn't seem as important. Still, they were in the lead for wins so far.

The day after the race Sarah received another note. It was in an envelope with her name on it, tucked into the back screen door. This one really scared her.

You've been warned. You won't listen. You're still poking your nose into things that are none of your business. Leave it alone. Quit asking questions. Stop bothering an old lady. If you don't, she might be the one who suffers.

Immediately, Sarah rounded up the boys and showed them the note. This was getting very odd. Who could possibly be threatening her?

"You have got to show this to Chief McCarry," said Rob. "This is the worst threat yet."

"Why? I keep telling you, he doesn't believe a word I say," Sarah said with disgust.

"Maybe just to cover yourself," suggested Rob.

That made some sense. Rob was right. Sarah needed to show this to the police, but before she talked to the chief there was someone else she needed to see. She went over the twins' house and told them she wanted to see Mrs. Gerard.

"You're so weird," said Megan.

"That's not nice, Megan," said Melissa. "It's true, but it's not nice." They went and got Mrs. Gerard and then sat down on the porch with them.

Sarah didn't say anything right away. Mrs. Gerard was definitely having a good day, she caught on quickly.

"Why don't you girls find something to do? I want to have a private conversation with Sarah," she said, firmly but nicely.

The twins were not happy about being dismissed, but they went into the house.

Sarah told Mrs. Gerard about the note she had received and about the other notes. Mrs. Gerard listened intently and a worried frown came on her face. But she didn't say anything.

"You know things that I need to know, Mrs. Gerard. This might be getting dangerous for me and for you." Sarah paused. "I need to know what you know."

"It's happening again. Threats, intimidation, danger. It's happening again."

"I'm going to the police about this. But I wanted to talk to you first," Sarah said.

"Yes, you should tell the police. Although, before, the police didn't do anything, only accused my brother." Her face sagged with worry.

"You really need to tell me what you know," Sarah said.

Mrs. Gerard paused again. "Yes, I think you're right. I do need to tell you. I wasn't going to. I don't tell tales out of school. I was brought up on that. But I can't let you be in danger. Not knowing is dangerous. I see that now." She got up slowly. She seemed unsteady. Sarah stood to help her.

"Wait for just a minute," she said and disappeared into the house.

She came back, holding the pile of papers Sarah recognized from the box.

"I didn't really know what to do with these. I didn't want to show everyone everything. I wanted to pick and choose. But that's not fair." She handed Sarah the whole pile. "There might even be something in there that I wouldn't recognize as helpful and you would. I'm much better these days, thanks to you. But I don't trust my mind. I could be missing something very important. You go through these. See if you can find anything significant. What difference does it make now? Everyone concerned is dead. You are a wise girl, Sarah. No secrets anymore. Secrets pull you down, and my family had too many secrets. After you finish with the papers, give them to the police. Let's get everything out in the open. This is ancient history. I don't care who knows." She gave her hands a swipe on her skirt as though ridding herself of something. And her face looked more relaxed than Sarah had seen it before.

"Thank you," Sarah said. "Not just for the papers, but for your trust."

"I should thank you," Mrs. Gerard said. "You've been good for me, Sarah."

"So who's Patsy?" Sarah asked. She had never answered that question.

Mrs. Gerard laughed. "Oh, you remind me so much of Patsy. I guess I did mention her name, didn't I?"

"Yes, you asked me if I was Patsy."

She laughed again. "My scrambled-egg memory problems. Of course, you're not Patsy. She was a little friend of mine. A winter friend. My age. We were inseparable. Well, that's not true. She moved away after eighth grade and I never saw her again. But she was my best friend. And she was courageous like you. I never had any courage at all."

Sarah picked up the bundle and said goodbye. She needed someplace to go and be by herself with what she hoped was a stack of answers.

She went back to her house and put the papers in a plastic grocery bag. Then she climbed up the big hill, walked to the tree house and climbed up into it. She settled down and read paper after paper, rereading some, putting others off to the side. It was a bit of time travel. She was back in the late 1920s and early 1930s. There were newspaper clippings, insurance policies, letters of all kinds, business agreements, even birth certificates and a marriage license. It was the legal history of the Steward family and plenty about the Harding family as well. The island hotel was not the only business the two men had been in. There had been other small establishments and quite a few investments and stock certificates that must have been worthless after the crash; someone had taken a black pen and made X marks across them.

All these papers put together told the story of two successful men who suddenly ended up in terrible financial straits. That much Sarah understood. There was plenty she didn't understand, though.

"How come you're up there?" called a voice from below.

She looked down. Rob was standing by the tree. She hadn't decided yet if she was going to show these papers to anyone else. The police, yes. Mrs. Gerard had told her to do that. But anyone else? Mrs. Gerard said she didn't care anymore.

"Where's Jake?" Sarah asked.

"Doing stuff for his mother."

"Okay. Come on up," She held up the papers. "Maybe you can figure out some of this."

They spent the whole afternoon there. If anyone had told her she would pour over a bunch of dry business and legal papers, she would have said they were crazy. But what she knew made these papers fascinating. They were the missing pieces of the puzzle that had begun when they found the bones.

The clippings were the most interesting. Paul Steward had definitely been a suspect in the arson of the hotel.

There were letters there too, business letters and personal letters. They made several piles: legal documents and business letters, the more personal letters, and articles from newspapers from all over the state. Rob read the legal stuff. Sarah started reading the letters and articles. Occasionally Rob would hand her what they had considered a business letter but which turned out to be a response to a letter Mrs. Gerard's mother had sent. She had been trying to prove that her son, Paul, was innocent. She had responded to any article that hinted that Paul Steward had started the fire and she got occasional replies. She must have mentioned the name Michael Harding, because these letters referred to that name repeatedly. There was no evidence that Paul had anything to do with the arson. He was never arrested or prosecuted. There were just rumors and insinuations. Sarah thought about what that must have been like for a twelve-year-old boy accused of arson. No wonder he became strange and left town as soon as he could. No wonder he disappeared, never to be heard from again. He was getting away from those terrible accusations.

Kerosene had been discovered on the hotel site. The fire had been started by someone. And the papers played up the fact that liquor had been served at the hotel. They didn't actually use the word bootleggers, but they implied it.

"Look at this," Rob interrupted Sarah's reading at one point. He handed her a paper. "It's an insurance policy," he said. "The hotel was covered for fire. And there's a letter attached from a lawyer. It's trying to convince Mrs. Gerard's mother to file a claim. It tells her not to worry about an investigation, not to worry about Paul having to go through more turmoil. It tells her to be practical." Rob pointed out key phrases in the letter.

"She never filed," Sarah said, catching his excitement. "Because of Paul, she never filed. And Mrs. Gerard says their family went through hard times after the fire. I don't think they ever got any insurance." This began to make sense.

"Maybe the insurance company went under like Mr. Mills said. This was the Depression," said Rob.

"That could be," Sarah agreed. They went back to their reading, more eager than ever.

There were personal letters between Raymond Steward and his wife, sweet letters she had saved. And a few pictures and early school attempts at writing from the children. Some of the most useful things they found were some letters written by Emmet Harding to Raymond Steward. It was like hearing one side of a phone conversation, but sometimes the meaning was quite clear.

You can't force me out. I'm not giving up my share. I will sell my half and you'll be co-owner with the very people you want nothing to do with. We'll see who's forced out then. In fact, I wouldn't put good money on your continued good health.

You can't go to the authorities. You're in this as deep as I am. If you want to cross those guys, it's on your head.

It was only a matter of time before the big boys stepped in. Don't tell me you didn't realize that from the beginning.

Sarah could almost hear the other voice. Yes, there had been trouble between the two partners. And she didn't have to stretch her imagination to figure out what it was. Serving illegal drinks, somebody wanting to buy the hotel at the beginning of the Depression, people you want nothing to do with. All this in the age of gangsters and bootleggers. What else could it mean?

Sarah had been reading these passages out loud to Rob. He agreed with her.

It was late in the afternoon when they finished. It had been both a depressing and an exciting journey through other people's lives. They were finding answers, but they were discovering more questions as well.

Sarah was bursting with things she wanted to ask people. But she knew she needed to visit the police with her latest note and the papers.

She hadn't seen the police chief around as much lately. And he was actually sitting in his office when she got there. Maybe he was getting as tired of her as she was of him. It did give her a little sense of unease, though. If he had been protecting her, why didn't he think it was so important anymore?

She showed him the note. As usual, he took his time reading it. And then he gave her his standard silent treatment. But she could see he was busy thinking.

Then she handed him the sack full of Mrs. Gerard's papers and explained what they were all about. He glanced at them, but didn't immediately read them.

"I'll get some people to go over these," he said. "This is really going to help. I'm glad you found these and I'll thank Mrs. Gerard for handing them over to us. But, frankly, I'm worried about that note." He did look worried. He wasn't glaring a bit.

"We can't let anything happen to Mrs. Gerard," Sarah said. "Who could possibly be writing these notes? Why would any of this matter to anyone now, after all this time?"

He didn't answer for a minute. He looked like he was doing some serious thinking. Then he said, "I think it's time I introduced you to someone. Come with me." He got out of his chair with a few grunts and they walked to his police car. He let Sarah sit up front with him.

They drove to the new motel on the road to Milford. They got out and he knocked on the door to Room 17.

It took a minute before the door was open. A tall man stood there. It was the same man Sarah had seen in the grocery store and at the club. The stranger.

"Miss Sarah Ramsey, I want you to meet Mr. Jack Steward," said the chief.

"Steward?" Sarah pounced on the name.

The man smiled. "I'm pleased to meet you, Sarah," he said.

"You're the island man." It was the voice she had heard when she was running away, except now he wasn't shouting and he wasn't hairy and horrible. He was a nice looking man, about forty.

"I don't understand . . ." Sarah began.

"Why don't you just let the guy explain?" suggested Chief McCarry. "It might spare a lot of time and trouble."

"Let's sit down." Mr. Steward gestured to a small table by the window and he pulled up another chair.

"My grandfather was Paul Steward," he began. "I've been wanting to meet you, but I thought I'd better check with the police first. I didn't want to frighten you or anything. It seems I'm pretty good at frightening people. I'm sorry I scared you on the island. I just wanted to talk to you then, too."

"Paul Steward," Sarah repeated the name. "Your grandfather was Mrs. Gerard's brother? Then you're related to her." Sarah was bubbling with excitement.

"Yes. She's my great-aunt. And I wanted to talk to her, too. But the one time I tried, I really frightened her. I was afraid she was having a heart attack. She really worried me. I've been afraid to approach her ever since."

"She'd love to see you. But I don't get it. You were living on the island in that little shed? Why would you do that?" Sarah had so many questions she wanted to ask.

"I'm a writer. I've always been fascinated by the stories my grandfather told me about the island and the fire and all that happened there. I've worked for newspapers for years. Now I decided I needed to work on the book I've always wanted to write, the true history of what happened on that island in 1930." He spoke calmly, and yet Sarah caught his sense of excitement in what he was doing.

"So what happened?" she asked.

"I still don't know for sure," he said. "I've collected a lot of information, but I don't know that it adds up to anything."

"You're the one who went to the newspaper morgue asking for the same stuff we wanted," Sarah said.

"Guilty."

"Did you know about the bones?"

"Not until you left that hint on my doorstep," he said, looking a bit repulsed.

The chief sat up, eyebrows raised, and gave Sarah one of his glares. But neither Jack Steward nor Sarah took the time right then to fill him in. Sarah could imagine Mr. Steward's reaction at finding a thigh bone on his doorstep. She actually hadn't considered what a shock that would be.

"But I did find out about a man who disappeared about the time of the fire." He said, leaning forward in his chair.

Both the chief and Sarah spoke together. "Who?"

"It's a long story and I'm not sure about the facts, or even if they are facts. I'm chasing seventy-year-old rumors."

"I've figured some of this out," Sarah told him. She liked the man. There was a little of Mrs. Gerard in him. "It did have to do with bootlegging, didn't it?"

"Probably. The man who disappeared someplace around here at about that time was a man named Lefty Grabosky. I don't know what his real name was. That's what they called him. He was some kind of a gangster."

"Was Raymond Steward in with the bootleggers?" Sarah asked, eager for more answers.

"No. But he allowed Harding to buy from them and he allowed liquor to be served. Way off on an island, he didn't think it mattered. Raymond Steward knew Prohibition couldn't last and he didn't think it such a crime to let a person have a cocktail. But then he was sorry, because he wanted nothing to do with the criminals who ran the booze." Jack Steward had a story-telling voice. He was easy to listen to.

"Your grandfather—Paul Steward. He left and was never heard from again. Why?"

"He came to hate this place. He didn't have anything to do with starting the fire, but people wouldn't believe him. I think I would have left too."

"Who did start the fire?" Sarah held her breath, waiting for the answer to this question.

"Let me tell you the story as I know it. My grandfather, Paul Steward, believed he knew who started the fire. But he had no way to prove it. When you hear his story, it makes sense. Paul had a friend, Michael Harding, except he wasn't much of a friend. Paul and Michael's fathers were partners and the boys were thrown together. Paul knew Michael was a liar. Michael had started a fire in a shed one time and blamed Paul.

So when the big fire happened, people just assumed that the boy accused of one fire started another. Except that Michael was the guilty one and the assumption of guilt should have fallen on him. My grandfather never got over the injustice of it.

"And there was more," he said looking directly at the chief and Sarah. "Michael had mentioned to Paul that a fire might get them out of the financial trouble they were in. My grandfather thought that Michael, by some demented reasoning, believed he would be doing his father a favor."

"How could that be?" asked the chief, who had been listening closely.

"Insurance. They needed money," said Jack Steward.

"There was no insurance policy claim ever filed," said the chief. "We checked on that."

"I know," said Mr. Steward. "That's another puzzle that I haven't figured out."

"Not so much a puzzle," Sarah said. "In those papers I just showed you, Chief McCarry? Mrs. Gerard's mother's papers? There's an insurance policy and a letter from a lawyer telling Mrs. Steward she was foolish not to make a claim. She hadn't wanted to because she was afraid of more investigations and more accusations against Paul. The lawyer dismissed her fear of putting Paul through more questioning. He was telling her she had to be practical."

Jack Steward's face lit up. "That's great information. That's just the kind of thing I've been looking for."

"It's your great-aunt who has the information. You should go and see her," Sarah told him.

"But like I said, I scared her half to death the one time I tried to talk to her." He looked concerned.

"You're talking about the Fourth of July," Sarah said.

"Yes."

"She gets confused sometimes. She thought you were her brother. She thought you were Paul Steward. You must look like your grandfather. But wait a minute. That means—you took the letter I found on the body." She almost shouted.

The chief turned in his chair. "You took the letter?" he yelled at Mr. Steward.

Adults can look shamefaced too. "Yes, I did," he said.

"You tampered with evidence?" The chief's voice was severe.

"I didn't think of it like that," said Mr. Steward. "I thought of it as finally finding a bit of proof. And then I didn't know what it was proof of."

"Hand it over immediately," said Chief McCarry.

Jack Steward walked to the desk, opened a drawer, and took out a plastic bag. It contained the leather case and the letter. He handed the bag over to the chief, who held it carefully while he looked at it.

"I'll take this to the state lab," he said. "You've wasted a lot of our time by not turning this in, Mr. Steward." He was not happy.

Sarah was thinking about something else Mr. Steward had said.

"But what happened to Michael Harding?" she asked him.

"He left, went with some relatives. His mother had died when he was little. They didn't have a cottage here. Emmet Harding and Michael stayed in the hotel when they came up. I don't know that he ever came back." Mr. Steward had that story-telling voice again, like he was reading from the book not yet written.

"But he did come back." Sarah said, with excitement. She told him about the family renting cottages until they bought the Steward place.

"Their name is Emmerson now," she explained. "But you know what doesn't make sense? These things all happened so long ago. Why is somebody sending me notes with threats now? I want to know is who's sending them. It wasn't you, was it?" she asked Mr. Steward. She knew it wasn't.

"No, of course not."

"Mr. Steward," said Sarah. "You know, we've been walking down the same paths here. I think we've come to the same conclusions. But what I want to know is where your grandfather was all those years ago when he just left?"

Jack Steward got back into that story-telling mode again and explained how Paul Steward had joined the army and fought in World War II. He won medals and was wounded; he made the military his career.

"Ended up a colonel," said Mr. Steward. "And my dad followed in his footsteps. I was an army brat, grew up on bases all over the world. Interesting life."

They talked for a long time. The chief was directing his glares toward Mr. Steward this time. He was upset about Jack Steward taking the letter, and he gave him some strong warnings about what was going to happen to him. There was something about his tone of voice that made Sarah think he wasn't going to follow through on that. Mr. Steward didn't look too worried. At any rate, the chief seemed fine with Sarah now. He knew she hadn't had the letter. She hadn't lied. And she have given him all that new evidence.

Before they left, Sarah made Mr. Steward promise that he would go and see Mrs. Gerard. She told him she'd prepare Mrs. Gerard for his visit so he wouldn't have to worry about surprising her. And she gave him Mrs. Gerard's phone number so he could call first.

"She's better these days," Sarah told him. "She wants to know all about what happened on that island. It seems to do her good. She will really want to hear about her brother and what kind of a life he had. I think she's always worried about him. And I can't tell you how happy she'll be when you tell her he was innocent of that arson charge."

Sarah couldn't wait to tell Mrs. Gerard about her brother's grandson. She went over there as soon as she got home. She was going to approach the subject carefully; Mrs. Gerard had almost fainted when she mistook Jack Steward for her brother Paul. But, when Sarah saw her, she couldn't contain herself. She blurted out everything that had happened. Mrs. Gerard's reaction was complete joy. Sarah knew she wouldn't wait for his phone call. She was already looking up the number of the motel when Sarah left her. Something good had come out of all of this, after all.

21

One thing still bothered Sarah and she knew she had to deal with it quickly.

Tommy Emmerson was back, earlier than expected. And Jennifer was going to go out with him again. Sarah couldn't forget what Kyle had told her about the way Tommy had talked about her sister. She had tried to warn her about him several times. But Jennifer just wouldn't listen. She had the idea in her head that Sarah was trying to make trouble because she was jealous, and she just got angry. Sarah didn't know what to do. Kyle had this great idea of family. He expected Sarah to be able to talk to her own sister and she felt guilty that she couldn't. So she tried one more time to give Jennifer the warning that Kyle had wanted her to.

Jennifer was in their bedroom, getting ready for her date. Sarah tried for a conversational approach by asking her where she was going.

"Why do you care?" Jennifer answered.

"Seems like an ordinary question," Sarah said.

"Well, it's none of your business," Jennifer said dismissing her.

This wasn't going to be easy.

"You trust Kyle Rearden, don't you?" Sarah asked her. Jennifer ignored her.

"Kyle doesn't say things just to make trouble," Sarah plunged on. "And he told me that he's worried about you. He told me Tommy has said some things about you. Kind of disrespectful things. He said Tommy does that, just to show off." Sarah was talking fast. At any moment Jennifer would start yelling.

Jennifer turned and stared at Sarah. Her face got red with anger. Jennifer was a pretty girl, but when she was angry her lips tightened and her eyes squinted and she wasn't so pretty anymore.

Sarah took a step backward.

"Kyle Rearden isn't even here this summer," Jennifer said, spacing her words slowly.

"When he was here, that's when he said it."

"Good God, Sarah, you are so pathetic." Jennifer turned and left the room.

Sarah had known this would happen. She had known all she could do was make her sister angry. She had tried. But she still felt guilty that she had failed so miserably.

The next day, when Sarah saw Mrs. Gerard, the older woman was all atwitter. She had talked to Jack Steward on the phone. They were planning to get together. And Sarah could tell that just thinking about it was doing her good. She seemed sharper and more alert than ever.

Later that day, Sarah went to the store across the lake and, of course, she had her usual chat with Mrs. Peterson, who mentioned how interesting it was that the bones had been found and everyone had started remembering so much about the hotel.

"Yeah, I didn't even know the Emmersons were descedants of the hotel people," Sarah told her.

"I would think all this dredging up of details is quite annoying to them," said Mrs. Peterson, leaning across the counter, as she liked to do. "Mr. Emmerson is *so* into his campaign. He doesn't want any scandal right now."

"So what scandal would there be?" Sarah asked, not understanding what Mrs. Peterson was getting at.

Mrs. Peterson got that look on her face. She was in full gossip mode. "He likes people to think that his inherited money came from solid business investments," she confided. "There's always been the rumor up here that it was speakeasies. He certainly doesn't want any hint of the wrong connections."

"Mrs. Peterson, you are a wealth of information. Why didn't I come to you in the first place?"

"Well, I like your interpretation. Some would say I'm just a gossip," she said with a smile.

Sarah decided to do her part in keeping Mrs. Peterson's font of information up to date. She told her about Jack Steward. It would be common knowledge in no time. And Sarah thought that was a good idea. The time for secrets was over.

So things seemed pretty good to Sarah. The summer was winding down and the pieces of the puzzle were falling into place. And Jake, Rob, and Sarah were still one up on Tommy in the boat races.

Then Jennifer went missing.

That very night she didn't come home for dinner. And then she still wasn't there when it was time for Sarah and her mother to go to bed. Jean Ramsey kept going outside to look for her. Typical of Jennifer, thought Sarah, to not even make a phone call, to think only of herself.

When it started to rain, later that night, Sarah's mother became convinced there had been an accident.

Sarah's mom called all of Jennifer's friends, and nobody had seen Jennifer all day. They tried to reassure her– Jennifer and Tommy probably went somewhere, to a movie, maybe, or they might have had a flat tire. Or maybe they went out on a boat and, with the storm coming, they decided to head for the nearest shore and stay put until it was over. Or they probably just forgot about the time. There were a lot of ideas.

Rachel Young promised her she'd keep calling everyone and keep her up to date. Then the rain grew heavier. There was thunder and lightning. The electricity went out and the phone lines were down. That wasn't unusual; the electricity always went out when there was a storm. Around lakes, storms are notoriously fierce. Lightning strikes are frequent, and thunder seems particularly loud. There was a certain tree in the Ramsey yard that got hit often. Lightning does strike twice in the same spot; in fact, it has favorites.

Sarah and her mother didn't even think about going to bed that night. Mr. Young, Rachel's father, came over to check to see if they had found Jennifer. Then he took it upon himself drive over to the police station. But he was told there wasn't much they could do right then. There were trees down everywhere and the police had their hands full. There had been several accidents. They'd keep an eye out and alert everyone to be on the watch for Jennifer. As far as they knew, there weren't any boats in distress.

It poured all night. The wind picked up and the thunder and lightning didn't stop. The lake was wild with waves and foam. Streaks of lightning lit up the dark water, which was eerie. Looking across the water it was totally dark, with only an occasional candle flickering on the other shore, and then suddenly there would be a flash of instant light, and then instant darkness again.

Just before dawn, the wind diminished and the rain eased off. But the sunrise was weak and hidden behind a sky of dark-gray clouds. The battery radio predicted more storms to come. There was still no sign of Jennifer.

Sarah went outside to see what damage had been done. The boats had been pulled up onto the land and they were all right. The raft was still there. Sarah's dad had done a good clamping job, and the lightning tree looked like it had escaped this time.

The screened-in porch had taken on water. They had covered the furniture, but the sideways rain had dumped a half an inch of water on the floor. Jean Ramsey was working the mop with a vigor that belied her sleepless night, grateful for any action that could take her away from her worry, even for a little while.

Mr. Young came back and offered to check with the police again. He said the roads were really bad, but he had four-wheel drive. This time Jean Ramsey insisted on going with him.

"I need to talk to them myself," she said. "And maybe I can call my husband. Maybe there's a working phone in the village. You stay here, Sarah, in case somebody comes by with some news."

They hadn't been gone fifteen minutes before Sarah heard a car horn out in back of the cottage. A dilapidated old jeep was pulling up in the driveway, honking crazily. It screeched to a stop and Hulk Norton got out.

"Hurry. Come with me. Tommy's got Jennifer. Come on. Hurry," he shouted.

"Okay. Wait just a minute. I'll leave a note for my mother," Sarah said, starting to run back into the cottage.

"No time for that. We might be too late already." He looked desperate—he ran toward her, practically tripping over himself.

"Too late?" Sarah stopped. "Too late for what?"

He grabbed her arm. "I can't talk to him. He's crazy. Hurry. I'll tell you on the way. But we've got to hurry. Quick, before he does anything to Jennifer." He started running back to the jeep, pulling Sarah with him.

"Please, I have to leave my mother a note. She'll be worried sick."

"We can't waste a second."

Hulk pushed Sarah into the passenger seat, ran around to the driver's seat, and they were going. It was a wild ride. Sarah was clinging to the door handle and the seat and anything else she could grab.

"Where is she? Where is Jennifer?"

"This is all so crazy. He's so out of it, he's gone completely insane."

They were taking such a twisting and turning route that Sarah couldn't keep track of where they were going. They passed the mailboxes, then swung left toward the lake again, then onto the road that ran through the woods, then back to Lakeshore Road, where it dipped down and followed the lake, and then back up to the dirt road that went into the woods.

Hulk seemed like a terrible driver. They swerved all over the rough roads. Or maybe he was a very good driver to be able to manage the car at the speed they were going on the muddy, slippery surfaces.

"Where is Jennifer?" Sarah repeated. "Why didn't she come home?"

"God. This is so terrible. Tommy's totally wasted. He can't drink. He's one of those people who should never drink. He's a whack job when he's drinking. He gets mean."

"But Jennifer, has he hurt her? Why didn't you get the police? Why did you get me?"

He managed a quick glance at Sarah and then looked back at the road. "Tommy's been my friend for a long time. I'm still hoping I can get him out of this thing. And I got you because he's obsessed with you. That's why he took Jennifer."

"Obsessed with me? Why?"

"Tommy has Jennifer in a shack by the canals. He won't let her go. He had some idiot plan to blackmail you into dropping your questions about the hotel fire. He was going to give her something, make sure she was out of it, and take a picture that would make you stop, or he'd post it on the Internet or something. Believe me, I didn't know anything about this or I would have warned Jennifer. He thinks he's saving his family, saving his father. He wants to cover up the family history so his father can be governor someday, and his father needs this election to get there."

Hulk kept talking. "Tommy's trying to prove something to his father. He thinks his father is disappointed in him. I guess he is. But Tommy thinks he can stop everyone from knowing about his family's past if he stops you from running around asking questions. It's insane. The whole thing is insane. Who cares if over seventy years ago Tommy's great-great-grandfather killed someone and his son covered it up by starting a fire. It's like a really bad movie. The dead guy was a gangster, for God's sake. Who cares now?"

"You should have called the police," Sarah said, trying to take it all in.

"This is kidnapping. Tommy would go to jail forever. "Let's just get him out of this."

"But if he's hurt Jennifer—"

"That's why we've got to hurry." Hulk took a turn so fast that even Sarah's seatbelt wasn't enough to keep her from swaying into the side window.

"Wait a minute," she said, grabbing for the door handle. But they were going way too fast to open the door. "You're setting me up. You're doing this for Tommy. You're doing exactly what Tommy wants. You're bringing me right to him."

"No, I'm not. You have to trust me. I won't let anything happen to you. I promise. I won't let anything happen to Jennifer either, if we're not too late." He gave Sarah a desperate look and, somehow, she believed him.

"Tommy Emmerson is the only real friend I've ever had," Hulk continued. "But I've never understood him. He can do good things, like he's always defended me from kids who make fun of me. But then when he gets close to being a nice guy, it's like he backs away and does something really weird. I don't get it. I've never gotten it."

Sarah looked out and realized that they were down by the canals. She could never have found this spot by land–she didn't even know there was a road that came this close.

They pulled up to a shack she had never noticed before. Or maybe this was a part of a canal they had never explored.

He turned off the motor quite far from the little building.

"Be quiet. Let's not let him know we're coming," he said. "Maybe he finally passed out. That will make it easier."

They got out of the car, not even closing the doors because they didn't want to slam them shut.

Sarah hesitated. "This sure looks like a trap," she said, starting to worry again. Was she being a complete fool? He loomed over her as they walked quietly toward the building. One swipe of that big arm could send her flying.

"No. I promise. But things might get weird. I don't know what's going to happen. Just follow my lead. Jennifer and you need to get away. I need you to distract him. I'll handle Tommy. And don't push him. He's so wired. He started drinking yesterday and–just don't push. I want this to end without any more trouble. Go along with me. He's my friend and I owe him, and he's heading for such big-deal trouble. Maybe there's still hope we can just get this over with."

He stopped Sarah with his hand a few yards away from the shack. He went up and opened the door and peered in. Sarah could see nothing but darkness. It wasn't very light outside either. The clouds were thick, and it was getting darker.

Suddenly Sarah heard a hoarse shout.

"Is she here? Did you get her?" She wouldn't have recognized the voice if she didn't know it was Tommy Emmerson in there.

My God, was this a trap after all? Tommy knew she was coming. He was waiting for her. Hulk had just been following his orders. How could she have trusted him?

Tommy appeared at the door, holding himself up by pushing against the frame on each side.

"Get in here," he demanded of Sarah. His words slurred and were hard to hear with the rain pounding against the roof of the flimsy old shed.

Sarah was about to turn and run, except that just then she heard Jennifer's voice.

"Sarah? Is that you? Help me. *Help me.*" She was sobbing.

Sarah did run, but into the shack, not away from it.

Tommy let go of the door frame and let her pass. She could smell him from several steps away. He reeked of alcohol, sweat, sour body odor, and stale vomit.

It took a minute for her eyes to adjust to the darkness. The shack had only one small dirty window. She located Jennifer by her sobbing. She was sitting on a camp bed, handcuffed by one wrist to a pole on the side. Her hair was hanging down in front of her face, and she was twisting around, trying to get free. Her face was blotched with tears; mud and dirt were all over her.

"What are you doing to my sister?" Sarah shrieked.

Tommy laughed. "Doesn't look quite so pretty anymore, does she?" He shut the door with a bang. Now it was even darker inside.

"She wouldn't even have a little drink with me. She wouldn't do anything. Ruined my plan, ruined everything. I thought it would be easy." His words were slurred together.

The room was crowded. Hulk was hovering against the other wall, and he took up a lot of space.

"Get me out of here," wailed Jennifer. "Make them let me go. Oh God, you shouldn't have come."

Them? Sarah turned to Hulk. He was letting this happen. He could get them out of here with one punch. She should have thought of that before.

"You wouldn't listen," Tommy said to Sarah. "I tried to warn you but you wouldn't listen."

"The notes," Sarah said. "You sent the notes."

He laughed again, a slobbering laugh without humor.

"But you couldn't have—one of them came when you were gone," Sarah said.

"Oh, I had help. Didn't I, Hulk?"

Hulk didn't say anything. The wall he was leaning against was the darkest part of the room. Sarah couldn't see his expression.

"So this *was* a trap," Sarah said to him.

Still, Hulk didn't say anything. And Tommy continued with his crazy ranting. Jennifer was pulling at the handcuff. Sarah could see it had already made her wrist bloody.

"You wouldn't promise to drop it, playing little Miss Detective, digging up dirt that shouldn't be dug up." Tommy flung his words at her. "Well, you'll stop it now."

"Or you'll do what?" Sarah asked, although she didn't want to hear the answer.

He laughed again. "Oh, you'll find out. The high and mighty Ramsey girls won't be so high and mighty anymore."

"Let us go," sobbed Jennifer. "Let us go. Don't you dare hurt Sarah. She never did anything to you."

"You didn't either, sweetheart, that's the trouble," he sneered at her.

"Hulk, what do you have to do with this?" Sarah asked. "How can you be a part of this? You're not crazy like him."

"He's my friend," Hulk said in a low voice. But he gave his head a little nod toward Jennifer.

"Good old loyal Hulk. Did you know he had the hots for your sister?" Tommy said, turning to Sarah. "He was going to get a turn. I was going to let him have a little fun. But that cold bitch wouldn't play. She wouldn't even have a drink. She spoiled everything."

This time Sarah was sure Hulk shook his head at her. Tommy was pacing up and down and wasn't seeing anything very clearly.

Suddenly Tommy walked up to Sarah and pushed her hard, making her fall onto the bed.

Then Hulk was right behind him. He grabbed Tommy's arms. "That's enough," he said, as Tommy tried to wiggle out of his grasp. "Sarah, reach into his right pocket. Get the key. Unlock your sister and run. Get out of here."

Sarah hated the thought of touching Tommy and he was thrashing around so much, but she found the key and unlocked the handcuff, and Jennifer was up and clinging onto her.

They ran toward the door.

Suddenly Tommy broke loose. Sarah heard Tommy and Hulk scuffling. Then she heard a thud.

She looked back. Hulk was down and Tommy was holding a big board. Sarah caught a glimpse of blood around Hulk's head. Had Tommy killed him?

"Hurry," she said to Jennifer. "Let's get out of here."

Jennifer was having trouble with her legs. She must have been sitting in that one position for hours.

"The jeep," Sarah called, and they made their way toward it.

Jennifer climbed into the driver's seat and Sarah ran around to the other side. The keys, thank God, were in it.

Jennifer started it up and jerked it backward so they could turn around.

"I can't steer this thing," she said. She was sitting on the edge of the seat, her foot barely reaching the gas pedal.

Sarah looked back. Tommy was stumbling out of the shack toward them.

Now they were jerking forward. Jennifer managed a wide turn and then headed toward the rutted road. But they weren't going very fast. She was trying to push the accelerator with only her toes.

"Just go a little farther and we can stop and fix the seat," Sarah said. She was watching out the back window and saw Tommy running after them. They needed to get away fast.

It started to rain again, the first little drizzle quickly turning into big pellets. The road was still slick from the last night's rain. The jeep swerved from one side of the road to the other. Hulk had managed to glide the jeep around the fallen tree branches. Jennifer was having a much harder time.

"Faster, go faster," Sarah shouted at Jennifer. She seemed to be crawling and Sarah could see Tommy still running behind them.

Suddenly Jennifer managed to put her foot farther down on the gas. It meant she was almost standing up, barely touching the edge of the seat, angled like a board against the seat. She couldn't possibly see much out the window.

They lurched forward and gained some ground. Tommy was farther behind them now. Then there was a bend in the road and they started sliding as Jennifer made the turn. Before she had time to recover, a fallen tree loomed up on the road right in front of them. She jerked the wheel to avoid it. It sent the car into a spin on the wet muddy road. They were going sideways down a small ravine. Jennifer and Sarah both screamed.

They hadn't had time to fasten their seat belts. When the car smashed into a pine tree, they were both thrown against the front window.

Sarah saw blood. She didn't know if it was hers or her sister's.

Jennifer tried to restart the car, but the engine wouldn't turn over.

"Get out. We've got to run," Sarah said, and shoved open her door. Jennifer was having a harder time getting hers open, but then she just climbed out the back and soon they were both running up the embankment, away from the road. They had no idea where they were headed. Just away.

The rain was coming down hard now and everything was muddy. They slipped and slid as they climbed the hill.

They heard Tommy yelling in the distance. Sarah pushed herself harder; Jennifer was right beside her.

They were running as fast as they could and, unlike Tommy, at least they were sober.

They reached another embankment and climbed up. Now they had a canal in front of them. They ran down to it— there was nowhere else to go.

Rushes, big cattails, pussy willows, and prickly weeds grew along the banks of the canals. But they were tall and thick. It would mean some cover. They headed for them. There was a clap of thunder not too far away. The rain swatted their faces, stinging. They were both dripping wet.

As they moved into the rushes, the weeds tore at their skin. They crouched down and made their way along the bank, hoping they couldn't be seen. Tommy was still drunkenly calling to them, but he sounded farther away. Sarah could hear her sister panting and she was hardly able to catch her own breath. They couldn't go on like this much longer.

Finally, they came to a place that had some trees and fuller bushes.

"Stop," panted Jennifer. "I need to stop."

Sarah did too. And this was as good a place as any. They both fell prone on the ground. It was only when Sarah was already down that she noticed the poison ivy, but she couldn't move and at the moment it didn't even seem important.

They only gave themselves a few minutes to rest. Then they swam across the canal and along the other side. The water was slimy with weeds and muck. The canals were not for swimming. When they got out and sat on the bank, Sarah could feel herself covered with filth. They both stopped and listened. There was no sound of Tommy. As soon as they could, they started walking.

"I know this place. I've been here. I think the lake's that way." Sarah pointed. "If we get to the lake, we can get home."

By now there were flashes of lightning. This storm was going to be as bad as last night's. They kept walking.

It was simply a matter of putting one foot in front of the other. After a certain point of being wet, miserable, and exhausted, nothing seems to matter anymore. Sarah felt like she had zoned out. She had no idea of how long it took them to reach the lake.

They walked the shoreline until they came to the first cottage and they stumbled toward it.

Sarah recognized the woman who opened the door. She just couldn't come up with her name, but the woman was the most welcome sight Sarah had ever seen. The woman grabbed Jennifer and Sarah and pulled them in and sat them down and got towels and was soon pressing cups of hot cocoa into their hands.

"Mrs. Sidney," Sarah finally remembered her name. "Thank you."

She was bathing Jennifer's face and putting some antiseptic on it. The blood on the jeep window had been Jennifer's. Then Mrs. Sidney took care of Jennifer's wrists.

She hadn't asked a single question. She seemed to realize the girls were too tired to talk. But she had sent her husband out for help, and it wasn't too long before the cottage began to fill with people. Jean Ramsey came and burst into tears when she saw her two wet and filthy daughters. They both fell into her open arms.

The next person to arrive was Hulk. He had an immense bandage on his head and looked surreal, like an Arabian Nights Incredible Hulk.

"Can I talk to you for a minute?" he asked, pointing toward the hallway.

Sarah nodded her head at Jennifer. She wanted to hear what he had to say, and she was glad to see him. She had truly feared he had been killed. They followed him into the narrow hall, which seemed even more cramped and claustrophobic when shared with Hulk.

"I got Tommy," he said, hurrying his words as though he didn't have enough time. "I took him home. His dad wants to take care of this. Mr. Emmerson will be here soon. Let him handle this with the police, will you? He's not going to cover it up. I'm sure you wouldn't let him do that, but Tommy needs help. He's in bad shape. He did all this for his father and it got all messed up, but he thought he was doing something to finally get some credit from his dad. Just talk to Mr. Emmerson before you say anything to the police. That's all I ask."

"He kidnapped me. He wouldn't let me go," said Jennifer. Her voice was angry and she was crying at the same time.

"Please, just listen, Tommy needs help. Do you really think he belongs in jail for years and years?" Hulk pleaded.

"I don't know," said Jennifer. She was wavering. Sarah wasn't sure she should.

"You're a good friend," Sarah said to Hulk. "Maybe too good a friend."

"I agree," he said to her, but he was looking at Jennifer. "I shouldn't have let this go on from the first minute I started to understand what was happening. I didn't want to hurt Tommy. But finally I had to do something. I'm sorry about what he did to you. I'm really sorry."

He looked pitiful, such a big guy looking like a lost little kid. He turned to Sarah. "I really didn't know what was happening when I delivered that note to you. I had no idea it wasn't just a joke about the sailing. That's what Tommy told me it was."

Jennifer still looked confused. Sarah didn't know how much she had even taken in of what Hulk had said. They returned to the main room where even more neighbors and friends had congregated.

Tommy's father, Leland Emmerson, came soon after that. He did a lot of talking to all of them. Sarah wasn't sure she had ever seen a grownup so upset. He told them that he had already contacted people and that Tommy was going to a special place. He told them that he blamed himself for what had happened. He realized how much he had neglected his son. Mr. Emmerson was such a dignified-looking man. It made Sarah uncomfortable to see him humble himself.

"My son will pay for what he's done," said Mr. Emmerson. "But most of it is the drinking. He'll never drink again. I'll see to that. Alcoholism runs in our family. We can't drink. Even my grandfather didn't drink and he sold the stuff, all through Prohibition. And it led to him killing a man, which he tried to cover it up. There. It's out. Our terrible secret."

"Not so terrible anymore. It's history," said Hulk.

"It was the drinking," Jennifer admitted. "It wasn't bad at first. The drinking changed everything."

"My son needs help. He needs a great deal of help and I blame myself for not knowing that. The police will handle this. But I beg you to allow me to try to keep this from becoming some big publicity thing where he suffers because of me. He's suffered enough. I want to make sure he's charged as a juvenile and that he gets help. That's all I ask."

Mr. Emmerson was a good talker. He didn't sound like a politician at the moment—he sounded sincere.

"The police will be here," he told everyone. "They got stuck in the mud. I had a chance to talk to them while they waited to be pulled out. But they will want to hear the story from you people, especially you, Jennifer."

And when the police finally arrived they did want to hear from everyone. Jennifer told her story, Hulk told his, and Mr. Emmerson told his. Sarah added what she could. Everyone talked at once. Everything was explained over and over.

Finally, the Ramseys were allowed to go home. Sarah couldn't believe it was only five o'clock in the evening. So much had happened. Conrad greeted her as though he knew what she had been through. It took a lot of petting to reassure him.

Jennifer and Sarah were tired and yet wound up. They spent the rest of the night just sitting and talking. They couldn't even eat much dinner, and by nine o'clock they headed for bed. Sarah could hardly make it into the top bunk. Her eyes closed instantly and she was drifting off when her sister spoke out softly.

"Thank you, Sarah. You came after me. I don't know what would have happened if you hadn't. I was such a jerk. You tried to warn me and I was too busy being nasty to listen. I'm sorry. I'm sorry for everything."

At another time Sarah might have felt smug, or vindicated. Now, she was too tired. She listened to the rain ease off and stop as she fell asleep.

22

By the next morning the electricity and the phone lines were up and running. Matt Ramsey would be arriving that very day.

What had happened was all over the lake, and Jennifer found it very embarrassing. She wouldn't leave the cottage.

Later that morning Mrs. Gerard called to see if the girls were all right. Sarah assured her everyone was fine.

"I wanted to tell you that Jack Steward is coming over here this afternoon and he's bringing Henry Norton. Did you know Henry was helping him with his research? They've become friends," said Mrs. Gerard.

"Can I come too?" Sarah asked.

"Nothing would please me more," she said. "I'm just so glad you're all right."

Sarah walked over to the Frasers' at three-thirty. The twins were sunning on the dock. She gave them a wave and went onto the porch.

Mrs. Gerard and Mrs. Fraser were presiding over a tea tray on the table. Jack Steward and Henry Norton were already there. Mr. Norton looked uncomfortable with the tea cup in his hand. He needed his thermos of coffee.

"Isn't this wonderful?" Mrs. Gerard was twinkling with pleasure. "Just imagine, my brother's grandson right here with me." She reached over and patted Jack Steward on the arm. "I never would have believed this could happen."

"And I have a new second cousin," said Mrs. Fraser smiling. Everyone had questions; some people had answers. The time for secrets was gone.

But Sarah kept up the small talk. She was waiting for someone.

Finally, she heard a car drive up. Mrs. Fraser went into the cottage to see who it was, and came back a minute later. Mr. Emmerson was following her. He said hello to everyone, introductions were made, and then he turned to Sarah.

"This was a good idea, Sarah. It's time we put our pieces of the puzzle together. I've been very foolish to try to keep things secret when there was no longer any reason to. But politics does that to you."

Sarah wondered, later, how the conversation would have gone if she hadn't been there. She asked many of the questions that sparked the memories that came pouring out of everyone. Most of them were things people had heard rather than things experienced. But in the end, it added up.

Of course they wanted to know what happened the night of Jennifer's disappearance. Sarah told them everything. They were way past holding anything back.

When she told them what Hulk had said, about Tommy doing it all because he wanted to please his father, Mr. Emmerson had to look away.

"My God," he said finally, when he had regained his composure. "History does repeat itself. That's exactly what happened before. Michael Harding, my grandfather, started the fire thinking he was helping his father, Emmet."

"For the insurance money?" asked Jack.

"Partly. That's what gave Michael the idea. But he saw his father kill a man. He didn't know Emmet had buried him. Michael thought the body was in the hotel. He thought the fire would cover up the crime, they could get the insurance money from the hotel and get out of all their troubles."

"It was a gangster, wasn't it?" asked Jack Steward.

"Yes. It was," said Mr. Emmerson, "And it was probably self-defense. But Emmet Harding was into so many illegal activities that he couldn't afford to be investigated."

"Did he tell you all this? Your grandfather?" Sarah asked.

"Not for a lot of years. But when he was dying, he started telling me some stories. He was the one who swore me to secrecy. I made a mistake by keeping that promise. He wanted to be sure I never tried to get the island back or any money from it. He really feared exposure, even after his death."

"He let Paul Steward take the blame for the fire," Jack said, his voice full of accusation.

"He said he would have come forward if Paul had ever been charged. I'm not sure that would have happened," said Mr. Emmerson.

"But even my mother had doubts. She always wondered if Paul had started the fire and killed his own father," said Mrs. Gerard.

"That's why I'm here," said Mr. Emmerson. "It's time to set the record straight. Michael started the fire. Probably Emmet was willing to let the thing burn down. He was so angry that Raymond Steward wouldn't sell and get them out of financial straits. But when Raymond heard that young Rose Bianco was in the building and went in after her, Emmet ran in too, trying to help them. So Michael, who only wanted to please his father, ended up being the cause of his death. Believe me, he lived with that his whole life."

"And my mother was afraid to claim the insurance money because she didn't want an investigation. She was afraid it would implicate her son," said Mrs. Gerard.

"Yes, but Michael did one good thing. After Prohibition was over, he saw to it that your mother got one of the speakeasies to turn into a restaurant. He was just a kid and he was living in Ohio with distant relatives, but he insisted that she get one of the properties."

"I always wondered about that," said Mrs. Gerard.

"My sister told me something yesterday when we were talking. "said Sarah. "She said Tommy never wanted to go to the island. Did he know something about the bones?" Sarah asked. She was looking at Mr. Emmerson, but it was Mr. Norton who answered. He had been silent, just listening. Now he leaned forward.

"He knew," said Mr. Norton. "Hulk told me he knew. Hulk didn't figure out what it was all about until last night, but Tommy was scared that people would someday find the bones. He didn't know where they were, just that they were there. Tommy told Hulk the story of Emmet telling his son he had buried the body just before he went back into the burning hotel."

"That's true. It was all in a letter that Michael left," said Mr. Emmerson. "Before he died he wrote it all out."

"Oh dear. Just like my letter," said Mrs. Gerard.

"What letter?" Sarah asked.

"I did withhold something from the box. It was written to me by my mother. I thought to keep that one little thing. But I guess it's all part of this story, isn't it?"

"What did it say?" Sarah urged her on.

"Pretty much what's been said here. My mother didn't know that Mr. Harding had gone in after her husband. She didn't know that or much about the fire. But when she wrote the letter she was sure Paul was innocent. She said she had convinced herself of that."

"You should turn it all over to the police," said Jack. "It's closure on a cold case."

"Sure, why not?" said Mr. Emmerson.

"I'd like to keep the letter from my mother. Would the police let me do that? She told me how much she loved me. We never said things like that out loud in our family. I'd like to keep that letter."

"We could make a copy before we handed it over to the police," said Jack Steward. "Would that be enough?"

Mrs. Gerard smiled.

"There's just one more thing," Sarah said. "The letter I found with the bones, what did it mean? Who wrote it?"

"I've spent a lot of time studying it," said Jack. "And I still can't figure it out. In fact, I've decided I'm not going to write a true crime book about all this. I'm going to write a novel, and then I can fill in the blanks. In my book, the letter is going to be from Emmet Harding to the gangster, and it's going to say that he refuses to go along anymore with the intimidation and threats. Emmet is going to have stood up for what was right. In the end, he wasn't going to allow anything to happen to his partner, and that's why the guy came and why Emmet had to kill him in self-defense."

"I like that," Sarah said.

There was more talk. But, as far as Sarah was concerned, the puzzle was completed.

As happened every year, the summer was coming to an end.

Sarah told everyone she had a new preventative technique for poison ivy. She couldn't believe she had escaped, and she told everyone that it had to be due to her immediate swim in really gross water.

Her dad spent two weeks at the cottage and things seemed to be easier between her parents again. Maybe it was her mom's new haircut, or the kidnapping. She would probably never know for sure.

The Emmersons left the lake for good. Tommy bequeathed his sailboat to Hulk. Sarah wondered if he let them win the last two races. They were the grand champions for the year, but the whole Tommy thing had spoiled it for them. It didn't seem so important anymore, not even to Jake.

When the Emmersons put their cottage up for sale, the Frasers put in a bid. They were surprised that it was accepted so quickly. Mrs. Fraser and Mrs. Gerard would have their cottage back. That seemed to Sarah to be absolutely perfect. Maybe Mr. Emmerson thought so too. Those two women were so happy, it was almost worth the price Sarah would have to pay. The twins would be returning to Loon Lake.

Which didn't bother her quite as much after Rob came over to say goodbye. The Ramseys were almost finished packing up the cars. Jennifer was going to ride with her mother, and they were finished and about to leave. Sarah and her dad were going in the other car, and he told her he just wanted a few minutes to make sure everything was turned off. He went back into the cottage. Rob stood there acting kind of shy for a minute. Then he asked her if maybe they could get together sometime in the city. This winter. Off season. A definite expansion of their summer friendship.

"I have a friend who's got his license already, and he goes with a girl you'd like. She reminds me of you. Maybe we could come over to your side of town and see a movie or something."

He was actually asking Sarah for a date. He hadn't asked Melissa or Megan. He had asked her. Suddenly she was the one feeling shy. All she could do was nod her head. She was busy thinking that Jennifer would definitely have to help her do her hair. And Jennifer would. Things had certainly changed.

He turned to walk away. "I'll call you in a couple of days, Ramsey," he said. "We'll talk about it.

That calling her by her last name, that put things a bit back toward normal.

She had one last thing to do before she could leave. She ran over to say goodbye to Mrs. Gerard.

Of course, there was a big hug and Mrs. Gerard told Sarah she'd see her next summer. Sarah turned to leave, not wanting to keep her dad waiting, but she happened to look out on the dock. She walked closer to the screen.

"Come here, Mrs. Gerard, quick."

Mrs. Gerard came and stood beside Sarah.

"Is that what I think it is?" Sarah asked.

"Oh, my dear. It is." She put her hands to her face. "The loons have come back."

"Well, one of them, anyway." They were both smiling.

Acknowledgments

I would like to thank:

The members of my writing group: Joanne Dahme, Diane DeKelb-Rittenhouse, Lisa Nelson, and those that have come and gone, for their years of support and critique.

Judith Redding for her production help and copyediting, the staff of Tiny Satchel Press, and Jessica at Bella Distribution.

And last but not least, my family: Dick and our daughters, Cindy, Karen, and Amy for their encouragement, help, and enthusiasm, and our grandchildren, Maddie and J.J., whose love of a good story is encouragement in itself.

—J. D. Shaw

About the author

J. D. Shaw is the author of six adult mysteries, including the *Ask Emma* series. *The Secrets of Loon Lake* is her first mystery for teenagers. A married mother of three, Shaw lives near Philadelphia, Pennsylvania.